TAHOMA
LITERARY
REVIEW

tahomaliteraryreview.com

TAHOMA LITERARY REVIEW
Number 15
Summer 2019

ISBN-13: 978-1-7331052-0-0

Copyright @ 2019 Tahoma Literary Review, LLC
Seattle ● California
tahomaliteraryreview.com

Tahoma Literary Review

Ann Beman   Prose Editor
Jim Gearhart   Managing Editor
Mare Heron Hake   Poetry Editor
Yi Shun Lai   Prose Editor

Bronwynn Dean   Layout & Design
Haley Isleib   Copy Editor

Associate Fiction Editors
Michal Lemberger
Stefen Styrsky

Cover Artist
Leah Goren

Founding Editors
Joe Ponepinto
Kelly Davio

Table of Contents

You can hear many of the authors in this issue read their stories, poems, and essays at https://soundcloud.com/tahomaliterary/tracks.

About This Issue

Welcome to our fifteenth issue. This marks the fifth anniversary for *Tahoma Literary Review*; we have been publishing new fiction, nonfiction, and poetry three times a year since 2014. A quick dive into our submissions database reveals that we've had the privilege of sharing 376 original works with you.

When Joe Ponepinto and Kelly Davio founded *Tahoma Literary Review*, they did so with some fundamental elements in mind. They wanted a magazine that was open to as many writing voices as possible, that compensated writers fairly, and that could nourish what we call the literary ecosystem: the network of writers, readers, editors, designers, and publishers who make sharing the written word possible.

Joe and Kelly started with those goals, and we—Yi Shun, Mare, Jim, and Ann—continue to pursue them. We remain committed to paying our contributors for their work. We pay those who make each issue possible: our associate editors, copy editor, design and layout editor, and cover artist (among others). We delight in heralding the continued accomplishments of past contributors and we remain committed to expanding the range of writers we attract to these pages, widening the spectrum of voices we present.

Of course, none of our efforts would be possible—or worthwhile—without someone reading these pages. We are grateful to you, our reader, for supporting TLR.

We are again honored to present an issue packed with memorable stories, essays, and poems. In this issue the elemental power of Nature feels especially prevalent. Characters consider their relationship with the natural world and the animals or plants within it ("On Contrast," "Crepuscular Behavior," "Heretic," "Hydrangea"), while the sky above brings visions of flight through imagination, physical effort, and technology ("Icarus," "Hup," "In the Skies Above Southwest Oklahoma," "Gravity Haunted"). Heat and fire also have a presence, as the desert sun and summer press down ("A Good World," "Sex Ed," "Summer Solstice"), or fire wreaks destruction ("After Reading Reports from the California Wildfires Before My Father's Overdose"). Water courses through these pages, too, as a storm ("Lake Reality") or a powerful current ("Passive-Aggressive Flotsam Cross," "Studies in Erosion").

Our selections contain another shared element, too: human nature. Throughout our selections friends, relatives, loved ones and guardians reveal their struggles with each other and with themselves ("Song of the South, Reprise," "Origin Stories for the Turtle Lady," "Because of Course: An Award-Winning Story").

This issue also includes three selections from writing contests with which we partner. First we have "Grandma's Letters," winner of the short nonfiction category from Ooligan Press Write to Publish contest. The other two award winners come from the Intro Journal Award program. Each year the Association of Writers and Writing Programs (AWP) chooses outstanding works of fiction, nonfiction, and poetry which then appear in participating literary journals. "Visitation" and "Dear Anhedonia" are our featured winners this year. For more information about the Intro Journal Award you can visit awpwriter.org/contests/intro_journals_project_overview.

Thanks again for picking up a copy of *Tahoma Literary Review*. We hope that our foundation of support, access, and community continue to serve for years to come. Don't miss the issue's closing section with comments from our contributors (including the cover artist), and join us on Facebook (facebook.com/TahomaLiteraryReview) or Twitter (@tahomareview) to share your thoughts.

TLR

TAHOMA
LITERARY
REVIEW

On Contrast

John A. Nieves

In the heat, sometimes, it is   easy
to forget. It is easy to   wipe the sweat and keep
talking, even while we are   panting, even
while every   syllable rediscovers
thirst. In the cold, things   are harder and like
gems, able to glint differently   at specific
angles. I remember walking across   this
field in February   with a thin crust
of fresh frost. I had   a loose tooth from a bad
fall and my fleece   was dirty. The crocuses
had just peeked   up and they believed
in the pale sun and progress. My boots   were wet
but my socks were dry. I knew   I was never
going back   south. The wind   sucked the fresh
powder a few inches off   the ground like the elegant
swish of a gown. Here, now,   on the humid porch
among the flies and talk   of plane tickets, I force
myself back to that   resolve. I will not   buy
the rot and darkness. I will not   let myself forget
how constant blooming   means constant death.
The promise of winter is the promise   of knowing
what the world will whisper   coolly in your ear,
what it will take   from your bones and your breath.
In the endless summer, though, the cost is stealthy—decay
does not declare   itself. What is   softest, ripest,
is closest   to death.

CREPUSCULAR BEHAVIOR

CAROLYN OLIVER

The delivery truck that hit Lorenzo gave me two big breaks.

First, the company fired the truck driver, so I tipped off my room-mate Max about the job opening, and he got the rest of my room-mates to lay off about both Grant and my bounced rent check. Grant was a three-foot-long lizard, a black and white Argentinian tegu, and also the reason my check had bounced.

Second, Lorenzo being out of commission meant everyone in his department moved up a notch, at least until Lorenzo's legs got unbroken and his right lung uncollapsed and he could see out of his left eye.

Like every other zoo I've worked at, this two-bit private Midwest-ern one-step-up-from-a-circus zoo ran on hierarchy so strict you'd think they were trying to impress the Vatican. You had to put in your time hauling beet pulp and hay, shoveling shit, assisting at vet calls, all while paying attention and hoping to make some sparkly observa-tion that would impress a senior keeper and bump you up the pro-motion list. At least I was spared from endlessly directing visitors to the bathrooms; I only worked the early morning and late night shifts. The morning after the accident, I passed my shovel to a bright-eyed, alarmingly young college intern and started a new rotation, one I actually wanted. I'm a herpetologist—an amateur herpetolo-gist, Debbie the office manager loved to remind me, since I don't have a college degree. I wouldn't even get an interview at any of the major zoos, but in a county still aching from the last recession while it waited for the next one, there weren't a lot of college grads to go around. After they finished their summer internships (a valuable line on the résumé, at least, and fodder for "challenging situation you faced" interview question), they skedaddled back to school faster than kids run when they hear the ice cream truck.

The last zoo—if you could call it that—where I worked closed with no notice; my boss disappeared with a few valuable animals and my chances of getting a reference. That's why they started me here as a janitor, in the aquarium building. I was pretty glad to have a job, though. After a couple months the keepers began to trust me, allowing me to help out with feeding half dozen Adélie penguins, four nurse sharks, tropical fish restocked from a pet store an hour away, and a sea turtle, Polly, that hadn't been laid in half a century.

I liked Polly. I learned her well enough to know when something was wrong. After the vet saved Polly's eye, even Debbie had to admit that I'd been useful. But no good deed goes unpunished; they promoted me to assistant zookeeper in the small mammals department, where I wallowed for three years.

Then Lorenzo got hit by the truck and I was finally where I wanted to be. Officially, I was the assistant keeper of reptiles, amphibians, and birds, reporting to the interim head keeper, Brad, who happened to be the nephew of D. W. Breck, who owned the zoo. When Brad chose to show up, which wasn't all that often, he'd spend hours in the office with Debbie "going over reports." I hoped that when Lorenzo came back they'd shuffle Brad to some other department and let me stay, so I worked my ass off. This wasn't a stepping-stone to a better position at the zoo; I liked Lorenzo fine, and wished him a speedy recovery. But I secretly planned, back then, to put away some money for a degree, and then get a job someday at a big zoo, a place with more animals, maybe even a komodo dragon.

I never got over my dinosaur obsession, or my first lizard, an iguana named Beagle. My mom got him for me when I was ten or eleven. He seemed small and manageable, but we didn't know anything about the kind of light he needed, and before the year was out his bones went soft and he died. Unlike my mother, he never complained. That's the thing about reptiles: they don't expect anything from you, and they offer nothing in return, most of the time.

After Beagle, I kept to reptiles in books and on field trips, when my mom settled long enough to enroll me in school. It was years later, when I was crawling out of a dark hole, that I realized I could find jobs where I'd get to be around the scaly beasts I'd loved as a kid. While I was in mammal purgatory, I kept tabs on the zoo reptiles and amphibians unofficially, coming in a little early or staying late to take notes on my favorites, like the python, Gerald, and the blue poison dart frogs. Now that I'd been promoted, it was my privilege to keep them safe.

The downside of the promotion: birds.

Now, unlike everyone else who saw *Jurassic Park* the summer before Lorenzo got hit by the truck, I'd already read about bird evolution. I said I love dinosaurs, and that's the truth, but I do not love that birds are related to them. You ever see a bird up close, or watch one of those David Attenborough documentaries on a big TV? The leathery legs, the gripping claws, those eyes that flick from side to side—those I'm used to in my reptiles. But cover a reptile with feathers—pretty or fluffy—and it looks like a costume, like something not quite at peace with its nature. Not to mention the flying. I don't like things I can't see coming.

Sure, ninety-five percent of the time if you leave them alone they'll extend the same courtesy to you, but that five percent comes into focus real quick when you work with animals for a living.

I didn't mind Brutus, the crotchety bald eagle; he was a real jerk if you paid him any attention, so I ignored him when I passed by his cage, only sneaking a look inside if I was pretty sure he wouldn't notice. I didn't like the brown ducks that swarmed me whenever I went to feed the pair of cranes, or Dollface, the insane free-ranging peacock, who used to preen in my path when I needed to move cartloads of supplies, especially when it was blistering hot or pouring rain. Worst of all was the aviary. The few times I got roped into picking up extra shifts I tried to arrange my visits for after sundown, but even then chances were fifty-fifty that I'd be washing bird shit out of my uniform before I staggered into bed. Those little fuckers were annoyances I wasn't looking forward to dealing with, but they were the price for the pleasure of working with animals I knew and liked, the snakes and the frogs and the lizards.

Laila, though. She was something else.

"Rochelle!" Debbie yelled at me as I was picking up the previous shift's notes the first day after the accident. "Make sure you see the cassowary at least three times today. And type up your report—Lorenzo wants someone to bring it to him in the hospital." Her voice was sticky-sweet and slow, like molasses, and I was afraid I was liable to drown in it someday if I didn't pay attention. She knew just about everyone in the county, and meddling was her idea of entertainment. I grimaced into the folder I was reading, but managed a bright "Sure thing!" before I headed out on my rounds.

In the six months Laila had lived at the zoo, I'd only seen her a couple times. The first was when they called all hands on deck during a surprise blizzard in early March, and a few of us slogged to the paddocks in the northwest corner, farthest away from the main entrance. Lorenzo and I shoveled a path to the cassowary's building, tossing the snow against the chain link fence, which was covered in green plastic to prevent visitors from peering inside at old D. W. Breck's latest investment. The bird was under wraps until her big debut in the summer.

"Want to come in for a minute?" Lorenzo asked when we got to the door.

I nodded, happy to take a break from freezing my ass off.

Usually considered temporary lodging for animals in quarantine or rehabilitation, the concrete building had all the charm of a cell. The cassowary had been in there for almost three months. Behind the glass I could see potted palms, and branches artfully arranged to give the illusion of a stand of trees. Lorenzo had tried to perk the place up.

I took off my soaked mittens, but the air was cold and clammy, and I wished I'd left them on. I blew on my cupped hands as I approached the glass. The branches blocked my view of her head, so that if I hadn't known a giant bird was in the enclosure, I might have mistaken her for a mammal, maybe a curled-up chimp, or even a small bear. Her black feathers—each long and thin, like hair, packed densely into a glossy coat—shimmered in the slight breeze from the heating vent above.

"Why isn't she up? It's the middle of the day," I whispered.

"Laila's crepuscular. Dawn and twilight. Like you," he teased. I felt embarrassed that my hours were odd enough to be remarkable and turned to go, forcing my fingers back into my mittens. Lorenzo was still watching her intently, almost willing her awake, I thought. "Where are the wings?" I asked.

"Too small to see, really." He pushed his hair out of his eyes and sighed, sorry to leave her or sorry to go back into the storm. I couldn't tell.

Laila couldn't fly, but God, could she run. A few weeks later I was signing off on early morning deliveries of frozen mice for the reptiles and a truckload of last year's apples for our long-suffering elephant, Archimedes, when I heard Lorenzo shout from the direction of Laila's building. I hustled over, curious, and swiped my badge to get inside. Laila's cell was empty, and the keeper's door was open. I went through, and found Lorenzo in the space between the exterior of the building and the paddock's perimeter fence, invisible to zoo visitors. He had an apple cradled in a lacrosse stick—a relic left behind by an intern—and when Laila got close to the fence he whipped the stick forward, launching the fruit all the way to the other end of the paddock. She was gone before I could get a good look at her face.

Picture an ostrich running—a gawky kid who hasn't grown into his legs, right? Now picture a professional linebacker, a big hulking barrel body on two legs. That was Laila. Head down, wings tucked, legs pumping. Taller than me—and I'm five ten before I put my boots on, tall enough to look down on most people—and maybe a hundred and fifty pounds of muscle. Hard to say, since you couldn't weigh her. Too dangerous.

Lorenzo grinned when she circled back to the fence, looking pretty pleased with herself. Beneath that barrel body were thick gray legs, pebbled and crackled like an elephant's—lizard legs, with big three-toed feet. On the inside toe of each foot was a huge claw, four or five inches long, that made me think of a goring tusk more than a talon.

Did I mention that cassowaries can jump?

Yeah, Laila could come at you blazing fast and then leap six feet into the air and land with those claws sunk in your skin, or slash an artery. Not even Lorenzo ever went in the enclosure with her. Sometimes I wonder why cassowaries evolved that way—who was out to eat them.

When I said I had to get back to my rounds, Lorenzo barely looked at me, just waved me off as he gazed at Laila, racing for another apple. Seeing his admiration for her speed and her strength made me think that Breck's plan could work. I guess that bastard got one look at Laila's claws and thought, "Velociraptor," followed by, "money." Can't say I blame him. He figured that promoting her as a living dinosaur would get even more kids than usual into the zoo on summer vacation. And it turned out he was right.

As I pulled the gate shut behind me, I found a group of boys—it was April, the week of spring break—clustered at a tiny hole in the green plastic, whispering about the "dinosaur bird." One of them, with dark brown hair and long legs, shivered in the sun. I gave them a wide berth.

That night I started calling around to different pet stores and suppliers, asking about their reptiles. A smooth-talking guy in Mason convinced me to put a deposit down on a tegu, and I marked my calendar for Grant's arrival in late May. I admit to being a little lonely, just then.

When I arrived at her enclosure, still annoyed about Debbie's orders, Laila was waiting for me, or it looked that way. Maybe she was waiting for Lorenzo. She should have been resting in the sun, but instead she stood inches from the fence, glaring at me with one amber eye fringed by lashes so long they seemed fake. She looked alien, or like a child's drawing of an alien: her face and neck were a shocking electric blue that shaded to turquoise near her eyes and ears. Her wattles were lava flows of red skin, and the patch of crimson at her nape looked like an open wound. Looming above her head, tapering down to her beak, was her casque, the feature that made her look more ancient, more frightening, than her bald cousins, the emu and the ostrich. A casque is a big wedge of skin-covered keratin on top of a cassowary's head, something between a rhino horn and a parasauralophus crest, dark gray and lightly ridged (striated, Lorenzo would want me to say) like a fingernail. Laila's casque—a good six inches high—was tilted slightly to her left. Lorenzo told me later he thought it had been damaged in transport.

I chucked a pear over the fence. She caught it in mid-air and swallowed it whole. I was about to toss a plum father away—standard operating procedure to get her indoors so her enclosure could be cleaned—when I noticed something, a small nick or a divot, in the side of her casque. Had it been there all along, or had she bumped into a fence or a tree? I noted it down for Lorenzo, then reached for the plum again.

Boom. I could feel the rumble in my spine, radiating out into my bones.

The sounds that came out of that cassowary normally were guttural, croaking. Unreal, almost. Nothing compared to that booming call, though; I swear the air around us vibrated. I threw the plum as hard as I could and left. The cleaning could wait another day.

Lorenzo had always looked rumpled and sort of underfed, but his floppy brown hair, big eyes, and graceful lope had saved him from looking like a total bum. Now part of his head had been shaved so the doctors could stitch up a big gash, both his legs were in casts, and tubes sprouted from underneath the grimy beige hospital gown that covered him. He turned off the TV with the remote when I came in, which I appreciated. I waved weakly and tried to smile at him.

"How's Laila?" he said.

I decided to bluster through. "Nice to see you too. All the animals are fine. That zoo in Arizona called again about borrowing Helium for their breeding program. How're you feeling?"

"Jesus, Rochelle, what do you think? Like fucking shit. Go ahead and recommend loaning the gila monster—she's in good shape. Now tell me about my bird."

"Your bird?" He glared at me with the one eye not covered in gauze, so I kept talking, deflated. "Debbie said she would send you my report. Laila seems to be eating enough, normal digestion." I made a face; cassowaries have an incredibly fast system, so normal meant diarrhea all the time. "She's getting exercise and hasn't stabbed anyone or anything. I think she's good to go for the move to the new space." Breck wanted her right in the middle of the zoo, in the paddock that had been empty since the giraffe died in the fall.

"But?"

I focused on a sagging balloon tied to an empty vase on his windowsill. "I don't know, something seems off. The first time I went to feed her she *growled* at me."

"Really low, right? I think it's a warning sound, amplified through the casque—"

"Yeah," I cut in before he could give me a zoology lecture. "And she's done it twice more." I shuddered a little. I could practically feel the echo resonating in my body, hours later, redistributing into jittery unease. I took a deep breath and shook off the feeling as best I could. "Also, speaking of the casque, something about hers looked funny to me."

"That's why I asked you to come over. I read your report and got worried."

"It looks nicked. Like she banged it against something. Could she be disoriented? I wish we could let a vet in there. Any of her former keepers mention her hitting fences or walls?"

Lorenzo looked down, fiddling with the tubing on the back of his hand. "That's the thing . . . there are no former keepers."

"You mean they didn't have a bird keeper at that place in California?"

I'd overheard the name in the office months ago, but it didn't register. Just another private "sanctuary" that'd closed and shipped all its animals—if they were lucky—off to places like ours.

"No, I mean she wasn't in a zoo."

I'd been hovering by the door, but now I dropped into the hard visitor's chair next to the bed. "You have got to be fucking kidding me. She's a fucking import?"

Lorenzo nodded miserably.

"How did you find out?"

"When they brought her in I had questions—I had an emu pair

in the last place I worked, but I'd never even seen a cassowary before. I pulled her files, but there was barely anything in there besides the legal paperwork, so I made some calls and finally found someone who worked for the California place. They never had a cassowary. Then I remembered Breck's Australia trip from the newsletter. I put two and two together. When she'd been here for about six weeks I heard Debbie and Brad talking about the plan, how Breck saw one in some asshole's backyard out in LA last summer and decided he wanted a dinosaur bird of his own."

"Why go all the way to Australia? Why not just buy one here, or get a baby?"

"Baby takes too long to mature, and besides, they're hard to breed in captivity. He wanted something fiercer. He wanted her angry."

"No wonder she sounds like she wants to kill me."

"Yeah."

A film of sweat covered Lorenzo's face, and I was glad when a nurse knocked. Grateful for a minute to think, I stepped outside while she did her business. I couldn't fathom the logistics of getting a fully-grown cassowary into the States illegally. Or the money required. Shit, one of my old roommates was doing ten years for jaywalking with two ounces of pot in his backpack. I could taste rage on my tongue, powdery and bitter, like I'd ground layers off my teeth.

"What do we do?" I asked when I came back in. Lorenzo looked paler, but tidier too. The new gown was patterned with tiny blue diamonds. It was the most colorful thing in the room, aside from the balloon. I thought of Laila's six months in a concrete cage.

"I just told you Breck ripped a wild animal—a dangerous, secretive wild animal—out of an Australian rainforest to make it his pet project. And you think we can do something about it. You think we have a chance against a guy with that kind of connections?"

"You're smart, you've worked there forever, they trust you. I thought maybe you had a plan."

"My plan is to make sure her life isn't a living hell. That's the best I can do. Actually, I can't even do that." He gestured at the bed, the room, his legs.

I took a deep breath. Small steps. "So what's the deal with the casque?"

"Maybe she hit it trying to jump the fence. Or in the dark she forgot where she was and whacked her head. Just keep an eye on her, ok? I know you're the lizard woman and whatever, but …"

"Yeah, yeah. Ok."

A week later, right before the local schools let out, we moved Laila to her new pen. Mike, the head keeper, and the best of the three on-call vets, Maria, supervised while I ran the operation, which involved tossing fruit into a small delivery truck and waiting for hours until Laila got hungry enough to take the bait. Her kicks made bulges in the side of the truck until it looked like it had broken out in boils.

I stretched my hours long, arriving just before dawn and leaving at eight or nine so I could catch Laila's active hours at dawn and dusk. In the hot middle of the day, while Laila huddled listless in whatever shade she could find, I hid from Debbie and everyone else in spare offices, logging my notes and drawing up intern schedules, avoiding the busloads of day camp kids and harried chaperones imported for field trips. The zoo had a few people on staff as tour guides and "educators," but in a pinch a wild-eyed teacher will grab anyone in a uniform. From the office windows I watched children hopping like chickadees, collecting animals for their scavenger hunts.

Sometimes after work I'd visit Lorenzo in the hospital. I told him about Grant and my lost iguana, and he told me stories about growing up in Montana: the clear dome of the sky that shrank or billowed with the weather, the snow that gleamed from mounds high over his head, the animals he and his father and sister tracked not for sport, but because they needed to eat. Together we started planning, imagining how we could bring Laila's lush, wet, Technicolor home alive in the vast middle of the country, where we could see the summer heat crisping the long grass outside his window.

Then one of his wounds got an abscess and his temperature spiked and he was sent to the ICU. I couldn't see him for a few days, and I missed our visits. Laila seemed to tolerate me better, but she was still growling at the interns. At night, as I read library books on rainforests and living fossils. I spent my time off in the backyard with Grant, chasing patches of shade and weeding Max's unkempt garden. I felt suspended between the part of my life I knew and the part that I couldn't see coming.

I was already grumpy when Mike Hurston found me tossing mangos and lettuce to Laila one early morning in mid-July. The day before, Debbie had called me into the office to inform me I'd be working a wedding over Labor Day weekend. The zoo made a lot of money gussying up the place with Christmas lights and twists of craft store gauze for people who wanted a "unique" wedding experience. Keepers had to be on hand to answer questions for guests, and some of us—always women—got roped into waitress duty or bartending. I hated working weddings, and Debbie knew it. I mean, the money was good—though I had to be careful about that, since my first sponsor had drilled it into me that a big pile of cash was a temptation—but it never seemed worth the hassle. And I'd have to trust an intern with Laila's feeding.

I felt Laila's rumble before I heard Mike's heavy footsteps behind me, and before he could get close, she stalked off with half her breakfast still in the bag, even though mangoes were her favorite. Mike watched her go, rubbing his eyes with the heel of his hand. He was a big man, and steady, batting away annoyances before they got under his skin. Privately I thought of him as a stegosaurus.

"She always do that?" he asked, waving at Laila's retreating form. I knew he meant the rumbling. Even though he was technically in charge of all the animals, Mike was a mammal guy, and mostly left the birds and reptiles people alone.

"No, not too often. Lorenzo says she'll quit it once she gets used to the place."

"How's he doing?"

"Getting better. Another couple weeks, I guess."

"Glad someone gets over to see him. I don't think his folks are nearby."

Lorenzo's dad was dead, but I didn't feel like telling Mike that. "Why are you out so early?" I asked.

"One of the pygmy hippos gave us a scare. Turns out she's pregnant. Maria's on top of the whole thing. And speaking of the good doctor," he said, "I need you to keep track of what the cassowary is most likely to eat and what stays in her system the longest."

"Any particular reason?"

"We want to be able to calibrate sedatives for her, in case she needs any medical treatment."

I thought of her tilted casque and the dented truck and nodded. "Sure, sure." It would be a headache, but Mike was a decent guy. I didn't mind doing him a favor.

The weeks-old Fourth of July bunting that swathed the wedding pavilion—known during regular zoo hours as Jungle Jim's Burger Joint—drooped in the heat. The bride was one of Breck's nieces, but given the lackluster décor and the cash bar, apparently not one of his favorites. He was somewhere among the guests, who were glazed with sweat, batting away mosquitoes and wandering off in pairs down pathways looped with Christmas lights.

I was stationed at the bar, watching as Debbie played hostess—through her display of charm and competence, she hoped to snag a ticket out of town, a job at Breck's office in LA—and offering weak Manhattans to the old ladies, taking the caps off endless bottles of beer for overfed accountant types, mixing rum and cokes for teenagers. What the hell did I care?

Around ten Debbie wandered over as I was gulping down ice water.

"What's that?" she asked, shouting over the obnoxious DJ.

"Water."

"Give it to me." So much for the charm offensive.

I handed the half-empty glass to her. She sniffed it and handed it back. "What? Did you seriously think I had a big tumbler full of vodka or something? I'm not a drunk."

"I know what you are," she slurred in her saccharine sing-song. "And it's not a drunk." The 'k' popped from her mouth like a grenade pin.

I pretended to ignore her, handing a glass of red to an older guy with lips stained purple. I started washing glasses so she wouldn't notice my hands shaking.

"You think nobody knows what you are. What you did. You're not special, even if people think you're so mysterious." Hanging onto the counter by her fingertips, she swung away, then tipped back toward me in a rush. "Like that stupid blue-faced bird everyone loves so much. No mystery there. She'll look like all the rest of them when she's running around after her little brats."

The smell of the soapsuds made me nauseous all of a sudden. "What are you talking about?"

She mimed locking her lips and swung away again, lurching off toward the dance floor.

An hour passed. An asshole wearing a wedding ring tried to jab his tongue down my throat, so I let him have it. By the time Mike showed up and asked for a beer, my feet were killing me and my ears felt like they were full of cotton.

"Why the fuck does Debbie think the cassowary is going to be breeding soon?"

He took a long pull. "Breck made some calls to a place in Alabama. They have a male and they're going to try it out. Bring him in around Thanksgiving, give them a few months to get to know each other before the breeding season. We pay for the transport and housing, and we get a bigger share of the eggs."

"You know she could kill another bird, right?"

"Yeah, I know."

"But she just got here!" He looked puzzled, and I realized Mike thought all of Laila's papers were in order. Shit. "I mean, how're we going to fit more birds in the space? It's barely big enough for her to run in."

"Preaching to the choir. I had this whole conversation with Breck, but he really likes the 'deadliest bird' angle. Says she's too quiet during the day, thinks he can train new birds to be more— interesting." The word curled up with his disgust. "Wants a whole flock of them so he can put up billboards and draw in more business."

He took another swig, gave me an apologetic pat with his big hand, then rapped his knuckles on the bar and headed back into the scrum. A bunch of little kids hopped up on wedding cake and past-bedtime euphoria grabbed at his arms and badge, like sparrows attacking a piece of bread. He crouched down to answer their questions. I got back to wondering just what Debbie knew about my life, how she got to know it, and whether she'd told Lorenzo.

I was one of the last to leave, scooping up the leftover fruit from the dessert table to bring to Laila. Beneath the midnight sky she was a wedge of blacker dark under the trees, until the moon came out from behind a cloud and her feathered body gleamed like the ripples on a slow river. I didn't want to wake her. Grant got the fruit.

The next night, Lorenzo and I were supposed to be celebrating his imminent move to rehab. He'd set aside his low-sodium chicken soup in favor of a piece of mocha truffle wedding cake when I told him about the breeding plan. He started shouting, and I started picking my cafeteria tuna sandwich into little pieces.

"That asshole knows nothing, absolutely fucking nothing, about these animals. First of all, the mother doesn't raise the chicks. Doesn't even sit on the nest! That's the father's job. This other zoo is just going to let their cassowary go for months and months on end? Fuck this."

One of his monitors started beeping, and the night nurse—Annie, neck long like a diplodocus—rushed through the door, giving me a sharp look before she turned off the alert. "What's the matter? You need another dose of pain meds? Your anxiety bothering you?"

"No, I'm fine." He winced as a pillow she was fluffing tugged at his IV cord. "Actually, yeah, I'm not feeling so great."

"Be right back." She glared at me again on her way out. I cringed.

"I'm sorry," I said. "Mike is going to agree with whatever you say, but in the end he's just as helpless as we are."

Lorenzo nodded, but he wasn't really listening. He was waiting, I realized, for Annie to come back. I thought I understood. Need is like that. Makes everything else around you—the whistle of wind through trees, the cold shock of water, the smell of sunlight on a baby's scalp—fade into background noise.

Annie came back with pills in a tiny paper cup, the pleated kind you pump ketchup or mustard into. She watched as Lorenzo tossed them back. "You finish that soup, ok? And the call button is there for a reason."

As soon as she left he spit the pills back into the cup. "I have a plan," he said. "But first come over here and help me with the soup."

I liked Annie, but I still tossed the soup in the sink. Then I sat down, for the first time, on the edge of Lorenzo's bed.

Nobody thought it was weird when I volunteered to work Thanksgiving Day; I always worked holidays. After I fed Laila in the morning—mangoes unearthed in the fourth grocery store I visited, an hour away—I spent the rest of the unseasonably warm day out on the usual rounds, filling out paperwork, leaving extra notes. After I visited Polly and Gerald and the frogs, I walked the whole perimeter of the zoo waiting for lavender hour. She'd be up by then, pacing and hungry. The grapes were sitting in the fridge, each one stuffed, like a cocktail olive, with sedatives Lorenzo had been squirreling away. And a few more things I'd managed to find with the help of some old friends.

Lorenzo is a good person, a good keeper. That's why I left Grant at his place.

An hour after I fed her the grapes, as wisps of cloud turned scarlet in the sunset, I walked into Laila's enclosure. She was still warm. The blue leather of her neck was soft, much softer than I expected, and her casque was even bigger up close, scarred with fine lines. For the first time I wondered how old she was. How many chicks she'd left to fend for themselves, without looking back.

At the service entrance, I knew Lorenzo would be waiting with a horse trailer and a pickup to take us all to his sister's ranch in Montana.

I still imagine it sometimes, that trip we didn't take. I'd drive for hours and hours, way into the dark, the air in the cab dense with the smell of fruit, Patsy Cline on the radio. I'd trail my gaze over his propped-up legs to the side mirror, watching as this part of our lives was winnowed away to nothing across the endless plains.

ICARUS

DARBY LEVIN

Father is building a flying dream.

He has been building it ever since I was too small to see over the high railing of our tower. He has been building it bit by bit, stitch by stitch, until it grows so big it envelops the whole room.

Every morning and evening, when we hear the guards' knocking, he mutters, "Quickly, quickly, son. Help me hide it," and we hide the dream out of sight. When I was very small, we would sweep the feathers under the bed mats, seal the wax into the wall-chinks. Now my father's dream has grown so it shades the room in daytime, and when the guards come knocking, we must pull it onto the roof above us, using a web of ropes and knots that Father has also dreamed.

Father is clever. He has clever old eyes and clever old fingers that have twisted themselves into knots of their own. When he has his bad days, which happen more and more often of late, his fingers curl like veiny, hooked bird-claws, and I must do the fine work, the fine dreaming.

On his good days, he works from the first pink of dawn without break. He will not take food or water. One moment he is convinced he has succeeded, has created his masterwork. The next he drowns in despair, tearing his dream to shreds, leaving the room's corners littered with feathers that I must sweep up before the guards come the next morning.

But when he is happy, it's as though he is already flying. "Look at them!" he says. The dream sits sleek and curved and nearly finished in the middle of the floor. "Are they not beautiful? Are they not perfect?"

"They are. When will we leave, Father?" I ask.

"Tomorrow, son. I only have to put on the finishing touches in the morning, when the light is better and my old eyes can see. We will leave tomorrow."

Tomorrow comes and I wake to find Father in the middle of the room, his dream torn around him in feathery clumps. He has not slept; his eyes are rimmed with tortured red.

"Father, why have you destroyed it?" I ask.

"It is useless, son. Useless."

"But only yesterday you said it was perfect. The pinnacle of your creation—the best thing you ever invented."

"I was mistaken. It was all a horrible mistake."

"But Father, you're a genius—the guards all say so."

He weeps and tears at his clothes. "I am no genius! Don't say that; never say that!"

"I'm sorry, Father. You are not a genius."

"Thank you, son. Now help me clean up this mess."

We sweep the feathers into a waxy pile as high as my chest. The bare branches we lean against the wall. I look at Father over top the years' worth of feathers. "When will you rebuild it?" I ask.

"Never. I will never start it again. We will grow old and wither and die here, just like the King always planned."

"All right, Father," I say.

But each time, the next morning when I awake, he begins the dream anew, bending the branches into a framework, sealing the feathers on with wax he melts in the sun on the windowsill.

When we hide the dream on the rooftop, it is not so much wings but a lumpy mass of feathers. It looks nothing like the white wings of gulls, born to cut air. I wonder if the guards notice: a curl of wax on the windowsill, a stray feather in Father's beard, the shadow of wings from the rooftop. If they do, perhaps they think it is nothing but a giant nest, the nest of the King of Gulls himself, who has made his home on top of this tower to pay his respects to Father.

Father sends me onto the steep slopes of the tower roof to collect more feathers. When I was small, he had to lift me onto the high windowsill so I could grab the roof-ledge and pull myself over. The first time he did, I was so afraid I cried for hours, sitting on the edge of the roof, frightening the gulls so they all stirred up in flight. When I finally grew tired, I fell silent and looked out to the air. Everything was blue and I thought I might go blind because I'd never seen blue before—just the gray tower and the brown guards and the dirty, ragged color of Father's tunic.

Below me unfurled the drop between me and the blue sea, and the gulls whose flying-arms Father called wings were tucked gracefully along their backs, lined with feathers the way my arms were with fine hairs. The sun burned a hole in my vision of blue.

Father now builds more than he tears apart. I know Father, and the gulls, and the guards. I do not know the island Father talks of, or the people whose names he mentions that he says will help us. I do not know the grass or sleeping on anything other than stone or the faces of anyone but Father.

I stay on the roof-ledge now, even when the blue sky fades to dark, so I do not have to see the dream unfolding in the idle of the room, like a gull-chick hatching from its egg. It is growing every day, growing and growing, and Father barely cares to hide it anymore.

"It is finished, son," he calls to me one day.

I am not sure whether to believe him this time.

But when I swing myself down from the roof-ledge, blinking in the sudden gloom of the tower, there it is. The dream and a second one for me, sitting fully finished in the center of the floor. The wings seem to glow, their lines curving back gracefully like a gull's. Father is a shadow in the corner.

"Put them on, put them on." He lifts the wings onto my shoulders, fastening the laces. "Remember what I have told you about flying."

I nod. The wings are heavy; Father's dream settles around me like a bulky skin.

"Don't fear now, son. Soon we will be far from here, on an island where the King will protect us."

"I thought you said the King wanted us to wither and grow old."

"No, son. A new King. A different King."

I pause. "Will there be a new sky? New gulls? A new tower?"

"No tower, son. And the sky and gulls will be far away. We will live on the ground again, with other humans, and everyone will know us by our names."

I have been no one for so long, no one in the tower of nowhere. I have always been so, but not Father. I do not like being reminded that Father has another name. I am not sure I like the feel of the branches on my back. The feathers are smooth and slippery.

Father weeps as he finishes, but after so many years of them, I know these tears. They are tears of joy.

"Soon, my son. We will leave this gods-cursed place behind and we will be free forever."

I jump and the dream catches the air above me, just like Father said it would. It fills with air with each strong stroke of my arms. The tower is below me and the gulls I stole from all those years are the size of the people-ants below, and the people-ants themselves are invisible.

I am stuck between the blue of the sea and the blue of the sky like one of Father's feathers trapped in wax. In the distance is the green of the island Father spoke of, weeping. It is a color I have only ever seen from afar.

Above me, the sun is the yellow yolk of a gull's egg, cracked open in the morning light. The air whistles past me, the way I'd always imagined it would if I let go of the tower's roof-ledge, except I am falling up, away from the island, away from the tower and the blue sea—and oh the sky and oh the yellow, yellow sun.

Lake Reality

F. Daniel Rzicznek

A freezing man toward the bow.
Beside me, toward stern, another
freezing in a tattered rainsuit.
A hard spray peppers our faces

while the fogs approach, steady,
curious as domesticated mammals,
accustomed to delivering visions.
Home, certainly, to bank swallows

hunting flies above the waves,
threading the green of the trees
while the wind wheels north
and late spring clouds pile up

more vivid than any hallucination.
This is the lake and we freeze,
this lake always and always moving,
the flooded depths below, still still.

~

Once a valley, now a lake, this lake's
enough to keep the bait-house lit,
grackles scheming for minnows
above a minnow tank left unlatched.

We see the rain a mile off
between gears of cloud and sun,
watch its drab tongues advance.
Mist escapes the horizon,

erasing horizon as it escapes.
Wind, at play, plows our faces
into wrinkles like wax cooling,
flashes of white inside the fog.

The sunken roadbed's sepia murk,
the watery sky above a ruin of farms,
no other world quite like this.
We head home. We curse the rain.

~

The rain weaves its cloak, draws
it over us. Nothing philosophical
here. Woolly strands of vapor
press a radius of droplets down.

The swallows arc after bugs across
wave-troughs strafed by rain.
The two wooded islands shudder
facing the gale. What a time

to be in a boat, living ghost minutes
of a self that rose in the darkness,
made water hot with electricity,
let the dog out and put him back,

made faith from the meaningless:
how blue sky becomes stinging rain,
becomes the mist, becomes how
precariously the waves are arrayed.

HUP

EMILY BRISSE

"The bar will be heavier than you expect," the instructor said. Three stories below, her colleague had mentioned this same thing. The repetition, spoken around the sound of her clicking hooks onto my harness, echoed like practical information I should pay attention to. But I didn't. I couldn't. There wasn't room. I stood, clinging to a slim railing, atop a six-by-three-foot board, surrounded by open air.

Two weeks earlier, a friend invited me to a trapeze class. Had I thought the experience through, I would have likely said no. I mean— trapeze? Leaps from great heights? Swinging upside down while hanging from my knees? I'd been ten years old a few decades ago. But it was mid-semester. I was teaching five classes of teenagers. Each night I toted home stacks of essays my two small children rendered impossible to grade. There were doctor appointments to schedule. A cracked refrigerator shelf to fix. A driver's license to update at an actual DMV. I didn't have time to carefully consider the circus. So a few days later, when my friend asked again—adding, concern in her eyes, that it would be good for me—I said yes, in the way one nods to a refill of water: to get on with the next thing. When the evening came, I drove to her house, joined a few others in her car, and let her navigate the dark toward a reformed warehouse in an unfamiliar part of town while I tapped a grocery list into my phone.

Upon entering the warehouse, though, I had to put my phone down because I'd started to shake. Sure, a little bit of nerves, I sup- posed. But I was mostly just cold. It was winter. My clothes were thin. I'd had to remove my shoes, and my socks were old. But twenty min- utes later, after the floor instructor gave a brief lesson on a low bar and talked us through a practice jump from a one-foot platform, my teeth still chattered and knocked against each other, like they wanted to leap from my mouth. My tongue felt overlarge, trapped, numb. As I climbed the narrow ladder, it bobbing beneath my weight, beads of sweat popped along my hairline. Once atop the board with this second instructor, I watched as she used a long pole to retrieve the fly bar from where it had been suspended. She motioned me forward, said, "Here."

There was a moment, before I touched the bar, where my body noted the thinness of the railing my left hand clung to; the thinness of the board, slim enough—as I perched on its edge—to curve my toes around; the smell of chalk, its grainy dryness on my palms; a cool draft hitting those beads of sweat along my neck. And then, in my right hand, the shock of both the bar's weight and its cold—as bright and deep as space. It made me gasp. It pulled me forward, out over nothing, the world of air I would swing into as soon as the instructor called out the word to jump: "Hup!" But first she called "Ready!" And somehow, as I'd been told to do, I bent my knees.

I'm not sure what matters more: the sensation of the jump—the bar pulling me down and forward then up, my body working to draw my legs in and over the bar, my knees latching, my hands releasing, my chest and head and arms and fingers swinging down and out and back up, my spine arching, all of me penduling through space so quickly everything blurred, went blank, a whirling momentum, until I tipped backward, dropping eight seconds later into a wide net—or the fact that I jumped at all. That, for those few moments, I was more body than brain.

I do not *not* think. Like many people I know, I struggle to slow down. I try to be present, but to live in our modern world requires a forward focus where the bulk of the 3000 thoughts the average person thinks each hour are about creating what comes next. On my commute home alone I am working through the next day's lesson, planning out dinner, deciding which route will get me to preschool with the fewest delays. Usually, while putting my children to bed, I can center on their faces in the darkness—the richness and fullness of my life—but after I have tucked the blankets around their bodies, I check the time, gauging how much of it is left to do whatever I have on my list before my eyes close in protest. It has to do, I think, with feeling prepared. Isn't that, especially as a mother, what I'm supposed to be?

So it is all the more remarkable that I slipped into that warehouse without concern or even inquisitiveness: that I just showed up. Felt my body shake without determining why. Let myself be led. Perhaps my being there seemed so fanciful, so improbable, that it did not register as warranting the kind of attention I gave to the parts of my day I could attempt to predict.

In any case, the lack of one kind of attention left room for another. As the night progressed, I climbed that narrow ladder again and again. And I experienced on that board the absence of choice. I stopped shaking. My muscles warmed, and in the easy bay around my tongue I felt myself hum.

"Why *hup?*" I asked the instructor as she retrieved the fly bar, my one question.

"Because you shouldn't wonder whether you heard *go* or *no*. Overthinking equals missed tricks."

Across the rig, the instructor from the floor now swung from his own bar. He had told me, when our feet were both on the ground, that he would catch me. All I had to do was reach out and look up. At his call, I bent my knees. It was a long way down, a long way to this person on the other side of a wide room, flying back and forth through the air. I'm a school teacher, not a trapeze artist. I didn't know what I was doing there. I still don't understand how birds fly. Don't tell me.

Sex Ed

Mathilda Wheeler

If Daddy listened, he would put down his paper. He would turn off the TV. He would look me in the eye. He would take off his reading glasses. He would not joke. He would not say, "For crying out loud." He would say, "What is it, Tilda?" And his voice would not be impatient. It would be caring. And if I said, "Nothing," he would say, "No. Tell me." He would know to ask, to keep asking. And then I could tell him. I could ask him. About boys. About rules. About Ted Sayer. About the poker game. About the "showing" trades, the "touching" trades. But it doesn't matter. I can't tell him. He won't listen. I just stand there.

Megan's brother, Ted, smiled at us when Mr. and Mrs. Sayer went off to their dinner date. "You want to play poker, Meg?"

Megan swung my arm. "Sure!"

Ted had the nicest smile, and he was tall and blond and beautiful. I was so jealous of Megan having such a perfect brother, I could melt with it. My heart was melting now, except, "I don't know how to play," I said.

Ted said, "We'll teach you, Tilda. It'll be fun."

It turned out poker wasn't all that different from gin rummy, except instead of playing for points, you played to keep on your clothes.

"We'll be a team," Megan said. "Every time we win, Ted has to take off a piece of clothing. If we lose, we each have to take off something." Megan took me into her bedroom to dress up. We put on necklaces and snapped barrettes into our hair. She had a lot of stuff. I draped a scarf around my neck and she put on a cardigan, even though it was pretty hot.

Ted complained mightily when he saw what we were wearing, but he grinned too, so I knew it was okay. The first thing he lost was a shoelace in his sneakers. This was funny, taking off my horse ring at one turn, then squeezing the penny out of my loafer at another.

Then Ted was down to his underpants, and it wasn't so funny any more. "I guess you two are going to win," he said.

But we didn't win any more hands. Even when Megan and I had two jacks, Ted had three threes. We ran out of little things to take off—we too were down to undershirt and panties.

We lost another hand. "It's not fair," Megan said. "You're a boy. You don't have two embarrassing parts to your body like we do!"

"Meg, you had a heck of a lot more clothes on to start with. Are you going to cheat now?"

We went into a huddle. Our honor was at stake. We couldn't cheat. But Megan was panicked at removing her panties. "I have hair growing down there," she muttered.

She DID? I didn't. But my breasts were starting to pouf. I didn't want to show them to anybody.

Megan pulled off her undershirt and sat there with her arms crossed over her flat nipples.

"Don't look," I told Ted. "Look at that picture." A huge family photograph was on the wall over his left shoulder. Mrs. Sayer sat with a younger Megan pulled in close to her side with the boys and Mr. Sayer around her. I wiggled my legs through the holes of my panties, and tore them off fast fast fast. Then I raised my knees and pulled my undershirt down over them. A big hole gaped at my neck, but my knees filled that, so I didn't think Ted could see anything. I felt numb with relief. "You can look now," I said.

Ted nodded at us. "Bravo, girls. Ready for the next hand?" He picked up the cards.

"No!" we both shrieked. "You won! We lost—end of game!! Now go away so we can get dressed."

"Oh come on," he said. "That's not the end—we play until somebody's totally naked. That's how you play."

But we wouldn't. I was so glad Megan wouldn't.

No one wore seat belts back then, not in the back seat, and there was plenty of room to slide, if your legs didn't stick to the vinyl. That day I was in the middle, Ted on one side, Megan on the other. It was hot and kind of stinky in the Loblaw's parking lot. Mr. and Mrs. Sayer had rolled their windows down before they got out and slammed their doors shut. "We need a few things for lunch—you kids stay put."

I could hardly breathe back there. No wind. Megan cranked down her window, but Ted was just sitting there. Sweat beaded on his forehead, then slipped down near his left eye. Even sweaty he was cute, but I was too hot to care. My own sweat trickled from under my arm and dribbled down my side into my underpants.

"Can you open your window?" I said.

He smiled at me.

"Come on, Ted. I'm boiling."

"Go for it." He raised his eyebrows and sat back.

Just like a sister. I rolled my eyes to Megan to share the groan, but she had stuck most of her body out her window, cutting off even more air from that side. I glowered at Ted. If he were my sister Lindsay, I would have dug my elbows into his thighs hard. Instead, I leaned over. The blond fuzz on the top of his thighs tickled my upper arms. I had to push into Ted's hot stomach to get a grip on the slippery window crank. Serve him right.

I slumped back into my seat, but there was still no air. Only the smell of melting tar and exhaust. Cars honked, doors closed, kids complained, parents snapped back. How long were Mr. and Mrs. Sayer going to take?

Megan now sat on the window opening, head above the top of the car, knees pointing toward me. Lucky stiff. Ted lounged, his knees splayed open, taking up too much space.

"Aren't you hot?" I said.

"Always," he said. A moment passed. We breathed together, blinking. He pointed to his crotch and raised his eyebrows. "You want to see it?" he said. I think he meant his penis. Did he really mean his penis?

"I bet you want to see it. If you show me your breasts, I'll show you my dick."

Why would I want to see his penis? I shifted closer to Megan's knees. I shook my head.

"Okay. You can see it anyway." He unzipped his shorts and pulled it out, before I could do anything. I'd seen my father naked in the bathroom once, but Daddy's thing had hair all around it. And I hadn't seen that hardly at all—we'd both screeched and the door slammed shut in my face. Ted slipped his penis through the hole in his white underpants: an oblong bit of silly putty, with a pink cap at the end.

"You can touch it if you want," he said then. "I know you want to."

Megan's knees were at my back. I shook my head again.

"No, no, it's all right. Here, touch it." He shifted close, grabbed my hand and brought my fingers to the thing. Soft and warm and boingy. It leapt up.

I grabbed my hand back.

He smiled. "Pretty cool, right?"

I didn't nod or shake my head or do anything, say anything. I turned toward Megan's knees, which were very pale and didn't have any hair on them. And I stared at them, and felt the rock that sometimes lodged in my throat get all big and hot and painful.

And I heard Mr. and Mrs. Sayer's voices and Ted humming while he zipped back up and shifted away, and then Megan lowered herself back into her seat and pushed me closer to Ted on the way back to their house. And I didn't look at him. Or say anything. I sat small in the center of the back seat and hugged my own knees.

A Good World

MARIO ALIBERTO III

The hangover is an aching knot over Gene Shaw's right eye, and the Texas sun glinting off the bleached plain before him pulls the knot tighter. His condensed view of the piss-yellow purgatory is barely tolerable through the cobwebs of his eyelashes. Parked along a lonely stretch of US Highway 191 between the towns of Del Plano and Ulysses, Gene reclines in the driver's seat of the company's sand-encrusted ambulance, trying to meditate on the sound of the idling engine.

"That one there looks like it's been blessed with more potatoes than meat, ya get me?" The boy sitting next to Gene nods at the sky beyond the dusty windshield, his palms turned up, cupping two giant invisible balls.

It's Gene's second day with his new partner, a novice paramedic with barely a dozen runs under his belt. When Gene doesn't reply, the rookie returns to chewing the tip of a straw tucked inside a soda-fountain cup, tracking the movement of sparse clouds through the windshield. The boy breaks the long lapses of silence by announcing what the clouds look like, vivid pornographic depictions of genitalia that Gene ignores by pretending to sleep.

In the distance, the road dips and rises for miles, the barren land at the horizon contorted in wavy heat lines, plains of cacti and weed, and no shelter. As the form of a girl materializes on the road, she comes on like a spirit, the steady measure of her gait evocative of a higher plane of existence, as if two separate realities have come to a nexus on the road. The girl marks slow progress. She keeps to the sun-faded yellow line dividing the two-lane highway, feet bare, arms out to the side for balance like a tight-rope walker. The thin linen of her white shift brushes her knees with each step, billowing forward. The straw springs from the rookie's mouth, spraying Gene's face with small drops of soda and spittle. The boy sets his drink in the cup-holder and shucks Gene's shoulder with an elbow. "Oh shit! Wake your old ass up. Look at this."

Gene pulls himself upright by the steering wheel, eyes alert, a practiced response. He rubs at a kinked muscle where his neck meets his shoulder. His eyelids assuming a half-lidded contemplation, he finds the spectral girl. She completes another five steps before he says, "Told you we'd see one of those doves." He reclines, picks up his cup of soda, and gulps down the drink that he uses as a delivery system for the mixed shot of bourbon that he likes to think of as "the hair of the bitch that shit on my lawn."

The boy pops his door open.

"Wait, rook," Gene says, turning his head so the boy doesn't catch a whiff of his breath. "Just watch. Can't do nothing yet 'cept call it in."

The boy shakes his head in disbelief, but he closes the door and puts the microphone to his lips. "Five-three-bravo to dispatch, we have—a—a—girl in the road—" He releases the microphone's button and looks at Gene with that particular dumbfound speculation reserved for the uninitiated. Everything about the boy is soft as a pillow.

"Tell 'em you got one of the pastor's doves walking the line on 191," Gene says. "They'll know what it means."

After repeating what Gene tells him, the boy returns to his slack-jawed gawking. A female dispatcher's voice comes from the radio speaker with a static pop. "Copy Rescue 53B. If confirmed, keep to policy."

If the boy hears dispatch, he doesn't show it.

Gene snatches the microphone from the boy's hand, and says, "It's confirmed alright. This one looks like she got heart, dispatch. We might be a while."

A pause, and then the female's voice from the radio. "I'll check you out of service until she drops."

The Texas sun meanders overhead without regard. The girl casts almost no shadow. Step after careful step, she carries on. Skin not far removed from adolescence, blistered and peeling. The bottoms of her feet blackened and suppurated. Without wobble, without hesitation, heel to toe, heel to toe. The line goes on, and so does she.

The boy never takes his eyes off her.

Perspiration has made the thin fabric of her dress stick to her skin, revealing the outline of her undergarments, and if there is fear of perversion in the paramedics' observation, she shows no signs of discomfort. Her face is placid; if she is too hot from the sun, if she is cold with fever, her features reveal nothing. Discalced, pink skin ferments on the tops of her feet, matching the skin of her bare shoulders, her cheeks, the tip of her nose; yet, her eyes are clear, focused, over the verge of a smile that never blooms. Her hair, straw-gold highlighted red by sunlight, a burning crown; from a distance, one might think her afire.

"She looks young," the boy says. "How old you think?"

"Pastor don't take in any underage kids. She'll be at least 18."

The boy shakes his head.

An hour passes. Gene moves the ambulance only when he has to, to keep the girl in sight. He chews bubble-gum flavored baby aspirin for his headache, the only kind of aspirin that doesn't upset his stomach, and he tries to sleep in-between moving the ambulance. The boy sits by his side, nervous sweat dotting his hairless face, even though they wait in air conditioning and relative comfort. When they drive by Whiskey Cabaret, a few of the jobless drunks in the parking lot congregate to remark on the girl's passing in obscene terms, but take no further interest once the show moves along. Gene is occasionally awakened by his own snoring. The low volume of the radio broadcasts the chatter of other ambulances, the paramedics of Rescue 53B left alone to oversee the pilgrimage of their charge.

The boy leans forward, hand massaging his whiskerless jaw. "How long we gonna sit here? She clearly needs help."

"No medical intervention. Religious freedom and all that. The girl's pastor says his doves got to walk their penance out, and we can't interfere while she can still communicate her wants. She needs to make it over the city limits into Ulysses. If she does, the church people will take care of her. Or she drops and she's ours." Gene presses a finger to the underside of his jaw, cracks a knuckle. "Church'll threaten to sue us if we try to help her before that. And the company will let you hang for it, because they warned you not to render aid while the girl can refuse consent."

"Let me talk to her," the boy says. "Get her to listen."

"Unless you're the Lord or her pastor, she ain't gonna listen. Trust me. Let it play out."

"This is so wrong," the boy says, crossing his arms and rocking back in his seat. "What'd she do to deserve this?"

"Don't matter," Gene says. "That's between the girl, the pastor, and their Maker."

"She's dehydrated. Sun poisoning. She looks like she ain't ate in a week. We're supposed to do nothing?"

A heavy sigh, then Gene says, "You ever hear 'bout baby birds that fall out their nest, and what happens if humans touch 'em to put 'em back? Their mothers abandon 'em and the birds die."

"That's a myth," the boy says.

"Is it? Don't know about that. But I know if we help her before she drops, the church will cut her loose for not completing her penance. Then what happens to her?" There's an aggressiveness in Gene's voice that he leaves unchecked. "Most of these doves' home lives is hell. Or worse. It's what turns 'em to the church in the first place."

"I don't care if they sue me. I don't have shit. I'm not going to let her die."

Gene waves a dismissive hand in the boy's direction. "We ain't gonna let her die. But we're also not gonna be the reason she's put out on the street."

"What kind of church does that? Don't sound Christian. She'd be better off on her own."

"Don't be dumb, boy. She done something to offend the pastor that warrants her making penance. She don't finish, she don't get no absolution. And what do you think happens to a girl who believes her body is made of nothing but sin?"

The boy tilts his head, glares at Gene from the corner of his eyes. "How do you know so much? You belong to that church or some-thin'?"

"I ain't got nothing to do with them crazy bastards."

"What makes you an expert then?"

The wind raises a dust devil, and the sand dervish crosses the girl's path. Her dress lifts and the white of her thighs is buttermilk. The girl doesn't slow, doesn't so much as blink, sand whipping about her. Gene says, "I've seen it all before."

Mile upon mile, the girl does not waver. She keeps her balance, keeps to the line. The few cars that pass give her a wide berth, slow-ing to stare, but they carry on. As the sun sets behind her, a blazing tip of smelt iron-rod dipped to cool, the sienna sky gives way to blue-black night, and the girl comes into view of the sign announcing the town of Ulysses.

Gene drives the van parallel with the girl, a token of admiration for her spirit. Tumors of translucent skin populate the girl's cheeks, like bubble-gum blown to their limit. He is close enough to see liquid sloshing within the boils, and he knows it would take only the slight-est prick of a needle to release the pus. The bottoms of her feet are black from tar and heat, and the tops pink to her shins; the girl's next step crosses the yellow highway-line at an angle; the step after misses the line completely. Her arms fail to maintain their rigid height, and they rise and fall in their struggle to stay perpendicular, mimicking the broken-winged flight of her namesake.

"Hell with this," the boy says, grabbing a leather kit bag and drop-ping down from his seat. The hard-packed sand crunches under his feet like the sound of desiccated insect carapaces as he rushes to meet the girl.

Gene rolls his eyes, and after taking another drink of his bourbon and soda, slowly takes after the boy. The sun has fled, but not the heat, and sweat bonds his shirt to his skin. He flexes his hands, tries to keep them from making fists.

To the boy's credit, he does not impede the girl's path. She takes three wobbly steps before the boy says, "Miss, stop. Let me help you."

Gene hitches his trousers up by the belt. "Don't touch her, rook.

I done told you. Let her walk it out. She's got to make it to at least the sign."

The girl takes another step and the boy paces her, hovering his hand over her shoulder. "Jesus, the heat coming off her. Miss, please stop. Let me look at you." He pincers her arm at the tricep, and she shrugs his hand off as if it is he who has burned her, and not the departed sun.

The sign is less than twenty feet away.

Gene clamps his partner by the shoulder and the girl progresses two steps. He presses his fingers deep into the boy's shoulder, between the meat and the bone. "Don't touch her. She don't want your help. Not while she's conscious."

"She'll die," the boy says.

"Our job is to make sure she don't," Gene says.

The boy smacks Gene's hand away, and rears back with his kit bag, teeth bared. "Fuck this."

Gene reaches for the boy, his other hand curled into a fist, when he sees them. A man and woman in white robes standing underneath the welcome sign to Ulysses. The woman is of his age and the man no older than one of the fraternity boys from over at Del Plano Community College. They are each scarred on their face, pink patina'ed craters from where the Church has burned out their latent cancers. Purification in disfiguration. They do not move, and the air is so still now that their robes take on the appearance of armor, and in their impassive countenances they may as well be statues.

It is only with a dim sense of awareness that Gene sees the rookie drop his bag and run back to the ambulance. The rookie reaches inside the vehicle and tears the lid off his soda cup and whips the remains of ice and soda to the dry ground. He fills the cup with water from a thermos and turns the chewed end of his straw over and stabs it into the water. He runs back to the girl, water sloshing onto his hand.

Gene sees it all happening, but he makes no move to stop it, like his destiny is to be a counterpart to the doves, an observer of some cosmic balance. He whispers, "No," or at least thinks he does.

The rookie presses the tip of the straw to the girl's bottom lip. The girl's lips, chalky white, chapped with flaky bits of dried skin, quiver.

Her mouth closes on the straw and she sucks, drawing water. Her reaction is immediate, spitting, horrified. She claws at her lips, her tongue, inside her mouth. Blisters burst and runny, yellowish liquid streams down her face. She looks at the boy, her eyes fixed, and her scream is unlike any Gene has heard before.

The pastor's observers turn their backs on the scene and walk side-by-side out onto the plain, silent as ghosts.

Gene rushes the rookie and shoves the boy back and the boy crosses his feet and spills the cup to the ground. The sand drinks the water in. Gene wraps the boy's shirt in his fists, shaking him so hard the boy's head flies loosely on his neck. Gene vomits curses, a roaring tirade, and spittle constellates the boy's face. Gene's hands slide up to the boy's throat, crushing his narrow wind-pipe.

The girl's scream dies and her legs go out from underneath her. She sits on the ground, her head between her knees, before falling onto her back to look up at the stars. She breathes, eyes open, her hands folded over her heart.

"You stupid sonofabitch. Get the wagon and prep a drip." Gene pushes the gasping, red-faced boy away. He kneels beside the girl and gently takes her hand at the wrist, fingers on her pulse. The girl finally surrenders to whatever awaits her on the other side of consciousness. They lift her onto a gurney and load her into the back of the ambulance. The boy and he work in tandem, pricking her arms with needles, draining fluids from plastic bags through tubes into her veins. The boy drives while Gene works to keep her stable. Her feet are red, swollen potatoes. He takes her blood pressure the old way, fingers on her wrist. Her body a furnace, and his as well. He palms sweat from his face. He wants an ice-cold drink of water more than anything. Even more than the bourbon in his cup. He can't remember the last time that was true.

Days and shifts pass, and on one of the emergency runs that bring Gene to the hospital, he checks with the nurses. No visitors. The hospital sent word to the pastor at the church, and as expected, he sent word back that the girl had been excommunicated. The Church owes her nothing, he says. The nurses don't have a name for the girl to even start guessing where to look for her real family. Gene peeks into the girl's room as she sleeps. Bandages on her face and arms, her feet wrapped in a cocoon of gauze. She looks older in the hospital bed than she did on the road.

The next day, between runs, Gene sees the girl sitting in a wheelchair outside the hospital, underneath the shade of the overhang of the emergency room entrance, a pair of crutches leaning on the wall behind her. Her hair bleach-white from her time in the sun. Gene's new partner, a quiet man, former military, wheels in a bleak heart attack case flanked by attending physicians. The stink of cigarette smoke from the victim's house clings to their uniforms.

Air conditioning spills out of the automatic hospital doors and goose pimples spring up Gene's arm as he stands over the girl. Her hair hangs over her face, and there is no sign she is aware the world continues about her.

"Hey. You doing okay?"

The girl doesn't move. She is dressed in gray sweat pants and a gray T-shirt, the standard clothes gifted by the hospital for those without. A square bandage on her cheek and gauze still on her feet, now wrapped over with tape. A shallow breeze ruffles her hair.

The doors whoosh open and a pair of nurses light cigarettes hanging out of their mouths as soon as their feet cross the threshold. They glance at the girl, then Gene, raising their eyebrows before walking the opposite way. Gene makes it inside before the doors close. The nurse at the front desk confirms the girl has been discharged. He finds a vending machine in the break room and feeds some crumpled bills into the slot. He walks outside and places a cellophane-wrapped turkey on wheat on the girl's lap and a can of Coke on the ground next to her wheelchair.

There's another call—there's always another call—and Gene meets his partner at the ambulance. His partner lifts his head at Gene in question, but Gene waves his attention away. After the run, a minor injury that doesn't require transport, Gene cashes in on vacation time that has piled up over the years. He drives his pick-up truck back to the hospital. The girl sits in her wheelchair where he left her. The sandwich has fallen off her lap. The Coke is unopened, a circle of condensation at its base. The girl doesn't make a sound, but her shoulders are shaking, and tears fall like hard rain onto her gray sweatpants.

Gene puts his hands on his hips, looks out at the road, and says, "Pastor wouldn't have you walk no penance if you was only a dove for a minute. And if you was a dove more than a minute, you know he ain't sending no one to come get you."

The girl lifts her head. The bandage on her cheek, wet from tears, has peeled away at a corner, revealing the color of an Indian-summer sun on her cheek. Her eyes are puffy, the whites reticulate with red forks. She picks at pieces of hardened, peeling skin on the back of her hand, and blood bubbles to the surface.

"What's your name?" he asks.

"Asenath," the girl says, voice dry as burnt toast.

"Go on and drink the pop. Sugar do you good."

The girl reaches down with a slender pink arm and picks up the soda. She struggles to lift the tab with a fingernail, and when the aluminum is finally pierced, the explosion of carbonation and fizz jolts her in her seat. She lethargically sweeps long strands of hair behind an ear, and takes a sip. On the bridge of her nose, where the skin is not peeled to the pink, dark brown freckles amass.

"That the name the pastor gave you? What's your real name?"

"Asenath," the girl says.

Gene chews on his lip, spits. He opens the passenger door of his truck. "Can't stay here. Come on."

The girl sets the Coke down next to the wheelchair and stands. She hobbles on the dressings encasing her feet without a hint of fuss. Gene boosts her into the cab of his pick-up, her crutches left behind. The girl asks no questions. He scolds her against picking scabs or peeling her skin, and she does stop for a time, but after a few minutes, returns to it, balling up the skin and rolling it between her fingers.

Her back straightens and she turns her head when they get on US 191 and pass by the large wood fence surrounding the Revival Church, the church's spire and giant gold cross ascending against a backdrop of clear blue sky. The entrance gates are closed and the girl sighs ever so slightly, looking out the window, fingertips pressed to the glass. By the time they pass Whiskey Cabaret a few miles down the road, the girl is staring at her lap again and picking scabs.

They arrive at Gene's small, weather-faded ranch home on the outskirt of Ulysses. The sun, as usual, cooks everything hot to the touch, and Gene burns his hand on the chrome door handle of the truck. The girl has trouble walking, and when she allows Gene to take her arm and sling it over his shoulder, he burdens himself with as much of her weight as he can handle. When he gets her inside, if she is offended by the dirty laundry piled on the couch, three empty beer cans on the television stand, and a litterbox by the door in desperate need of emptying, she doesn't show it. The girl limps around the living room, using the walls to help with her balance. Gene takes an armful of clothes from the couch and dumps them onto the floor. She sits, folding her hands neatly in her lap. He tidies up the papers, the beer cans, and a few microwave burrito wrappers from a small table, and tosses them into the trash can under the sink in the kitchen. He opens the refrigerator, sniffs at a jug of expired milk. Shelves stocked with too much beer for one person. He fills a plastic cup with water and microwaves a frozen pizza that he cuts in half and puts on two paper plates. He takes a beer from the fridge, promising whoever listens on the other end of his thoughts he'll have just the one.

When he reenters the living room with the girl's plate of food and her cup of water, she is standing, looking at a picture frame hung on the wall to the left of the television. "I know this girl," she says. A faded photograph of a teenage brunette in braids, dimples deep as wells, the girl saddleback a brown mare, and Gene, before his hairline signaled a full retreat, holding the lead. The sun shines behind them, giving off a dazzling starburst with slices of blues and reds above the girl's brilliant smile. Her arm in a white hard cast and the small ink of writing decorating it. A small red heart. "She hangs around outside the church fence sometimes. I think her name is Keren. Some of the other doves know her."

Gene sets the plate and cup on the table gently. A tremor passes through his hands. He hides them in the pockets of his slacks and rocks back on his heels. "Her name's Lara. Eat something. Before it gets cold." He retrieves his food and his beer from the kitchen and sits on one side of the couch, leaving plenty of room for the girl. She studies the picture, as if there is some relevant knowledge to be imparted from something so long ago. His beer is empty before he takes his first bite of food.

The girl looks back over her shoulder at Gene, the bandage falling away from her face, exposing her burnt skin. "Pretty sure her name's Keren."

They eat their supper watching the Texas Rangers lose a home game to the Tampa Bay Rays in thirteen innings. When it's time to turn in, Gene offers the girl his bed, intending to sleep on the couch, but the girl refuses. He has broken his promise and drank his usual amount of beer, and she has not expanded farther than the single cushion of the couch. His insistence that she take his room is met with refusal, and he can feel the kindness of his offer turning sour. He drinks another beer before turning in, and as he lies on his back in bed, his hands work against each other, cracking his knuckles. He taps the bones of his fist against his jaw, eyes closed, listening to the rushing blood inside his body until he passes out.

In the morning, he is surprised to find the girl sleeping peacefully where he left her, the brindle cat he sometimes forgets to feed curled in a ball against her bandaged feet. She lies across two of the three cushions of the couch, her knees pulled up beneath a blanket. He changes her dressings, applies ointment to burns, and marvels at how little the girl flinches. She fits into some of Lara's old clothes. He schedules two weeks off from work. In their time together, they watch more Texas Ranger baseball and eat barbecue. At night, he drinks until he locks himself in his room. During the day, he cleans the house in increments, starting with the living room. The girl watches him from the couch at first, a refuge of three cushions she has made her own, until she eventually pitches in, dusting everything she can reach with some of Gene's old socks. The house begins to smell of lemon Pledge. The girl says grace at every meal, and more than once, when she thinks she is alone, he overhears her singing old hymns in a mournful timbre that ignites within him a deep regret at having abandoned religion so long ago. After hearing the girl's version of "Amazing Grace," he empties every bottle of beer from his refrigerator into the sink.

Many days pass the same, the girl taking on more small chores, helping Gene prep when he cooks, washing dishes after. One night after dinner, when the brightest stars are close enough to burn the tips of fingers pointing to their beauty, Gene leans back in a chair in the driveway, using a stick to poke coals on the barbecue that have long ago become fossil ash. Grease from the burgers he cooked for dinner stain the concrete beneath the grill and a line of brown ants from the grassless front yard dips into the shiny pools. The girl sits next to Gene, her feet resting on their heels, fresh pink skin shining beneath the ointment she applies with delicate fingers.

Gene tosses the stick away and leans forward, resting his arms on his knees. His hands yearn for action, for idle distraction, to tear the label off a beer. He wipes sweat from his palms on his jeans. "Let me ask you. Were you ever happy there?"

The girl's smile is one of obsession, the madness of religion. "Oh, yes. The pastor is very kind. And the other doves—it's nothing but love. We're all so blessed."

Gene shakes his head. "Not at the church. Whatever home you had before. I assume you had a family. Were you happy with them?"

"The only true happiness is found in God." With her hair tied up high on her head, the burns on her cheeks are exposed, the dead skin crisp around the edges. She applies a dab of ointment to her face.

Gene says, "You have to miss them. I can take you to them. I'm sure they'd take you in."

"Which them?"

"Your mother. Your father."

"I never missed them a day in my life."

"That can't be right."

The girl rolls her eyes, continuing to slather her wounds with the ointment.

Gene says, "You try forgiving them for whatever they done?"

"You wouldn't if they'd done to you what they done to me."

"I might. I just might." His fingers dance on his thighs, and he rocks back in his chair, the metal creaking with the strain. "You won't forgive them, but you can forgive a pastor who put you out in the sun and gave you all them scars?"

"I was the one who needed to be forgiven, not him."

"What'd you do that was so wrong that he'd put you out on a road to be cooked?"

The girl gazes down at her arms, the shine of the ointment on her burns. "There can be no forgiveness without penance."

Gene collects moisture from between his teeth with his tongue, and spits dryly onto the sand. He fills his chest with air and turns his face up to the night.

She says, "You looking at the stars, or what's beyond?"

"There ain't nothing beyond."

The girl caps the ointment and tucks the tube under a leg. "Oh, that's not true. You should go to the public service on Sundays. If you listen to the pastor, he'll have you seeing all the Lord's miracles. There won't be nowhere you look that you won't see God."

"Oh yeah? That so? Where have you seen God?"

The girl shifts closer, the metal legs of the folding chair scraping concrete. "I saw him the other day. On my walk."

"That was heat stroke and delirium." Gene tries to lighten the blow by smiling, but it feels more like a sneer, and maybe that's all it is.

The girl's blue eyes catch all the starlight, and for a moment, they hold within them the promise of great revelation. "I saw him standing over me. After I stopped walking, and I lay on the sand. I knew I had failed, and since I didn't complete my penance, I knew I'd be cast out. But then I saw him. He wore a white robe like we doves do. He looked down on me, and he was glowing. And right then, I knew he would never abandon me. That I was saved."

Gene steeples his hands before his lips, drawing a deep breath. "Listen to me. You know how long I've been working an ambulance? Twenty years. Seen a lot of people take their last breath under my care. A few of them I've brought back. Brought 'em back like the resurrection in the book come to pass before my very eyes. You want to guess how many people told me about Jesus when they come back? Not a one. I'll tell you what they do. They cry for their mommas like babes in the crib, and if they had seen Jesus, they wasn't impressed enough to talk about him."

A sympathetic smile alights on the girl's face. "You shouldn't say that. I'll take you to the church on Sunday. Even failed doves like me can go to the public services. Just listen to the pastor's sermon—"

"I don't want no words from that sonofabitch. And you might as well forget about going back. You know that's foolishness." There's a harshness in his tone, and when he sees no reaction from the girl, he clears his throat, and says, "You can stay here as long as you like. Until you're ready to go home."

"I'll stay until I see another sign," she says. "Maybe you'll see one too. Why don't you pray with me?"

"I don't do that."

"Did Keren pray?"

"I don't know no Keren. My daughter's name is Lara. She left me to take up with them doves a long time ago. I'm no perfect father. Never pretended to be. But I ain't never hurt her equal to one of them walks the pastor sent her on."

The girl arched an eyebrow. "But you hurt her?"

"There ain't nothing easy about being a father. We all screw up our kids. Don't mean we don't love 'em. After Lara split, I let her have her time at the church, gave her space. Thought a touch of faith might do her good. Then I saw her walking the line and I tried to help her the same way that boy I was training tried to help you. Church threw her out, same as you. I ain't seen or heard from her in forever."

"She didn't need your help. I didn't need your help. Jesus watches over us. I bet he was looking out for her same as he was me."

"You think so, girl?"

The girl lifts her head to the stars, and for the first time, her smile fades. "Why won't you say my name?"

"I would, if I knew it."

"Asenath."

He stands so quickly the chair falls over, metal clapping on concrete, and he kicks the barbecue across the driveway, a plume of ash erupting into the air, a gray cloud descending slowly about them.

A gulf of silence exists between them the next day. The girl stays on the couch stroking the traitorous cat as Gene futzes around the house. The tension carries over into the evening, and over a meal of hot dogs and tater tots he tries to make amends, offering to have one of the surgeons he knows take a look at grafting her burns, most of which will assuredly scar.

With a full mouth, and a bit of mustard clinging to her upper lip, she says, "I'll keep them. Plenty of doves have them."

"You ain't a dove no more," Gene says, not unkindly.

"They're my scars. I earned them. And I earned a name." The girl swallows her food and doesn't touch another bite.

A couple of days go by and he no longer catches her singing, and dust grows like fur over all his things. She rarely leaves her cushion on the couch. It is on her third day of silence that Gene stocks the refrigerator with beer. The girl is curled up on the couch, knees drawn to her chest. The cat leaps from her lap, hisses, and scatters as Gene approaches. He crouches before her, grabs the remote, and mutes the baseball game. He sets an unopened beer bottle on the table and takes a slug from the open beer in his hand. The sun sinks slowly behind the blinds, and the shadows of the room dance around them as if possessed by ritual.

"I've been thinking," Gene says, swirling the beer in his bottle in tiny circles.

The girl draws her knees up closer to her body, tucks her chin between them.

Gene takes a drink. "You say you saw God out there on 191. But I'm thinking, my medic shirt is white. And I was standing over you, saving your life. You had heatstroke. Hallucinating. I'm thinking I'm the closest thing to God you ever seen."

The girl picks at the remnants of a scab on the top of her foot and a pinhole sized circle of blood forms. "The only stitch of God in this house is what I brought with me."

Gene takes another drink, and reaches out and draws a lock of blonde hair away from her face, rubbing it between fingers and thumb. "Why don't you let me take you back to your parents? I can do that. You can go home."

"I am going home. I'm going to tell the pastor what I saw and he'll take me back. I'll be a dove again."

The girl's hair winds around his fingers. He pulls it close to his nose, sniffs, but he drank too much, and his sense of smell is gone. "He won't. You know it. You could produce Jesus himself and that pastor won't take back a broken dove. I know it. I tried for Lara. I begged him. I begged him to take her back for what I done. Wasn't her fault I tried to help her. She didn't ask for it. I told him all that, but he didn't care."

"I'm going back," the girl says.

"You can go home. Your parents will take you, I swear it. Just tell me your name and I'll find them."

"I'm never going back there. I'm going back to the church."

"What's your name?" he asks.

"Asenath," the girl says.

He twists the girl's hair tightly into a fist, and her head bows as he pulls. "Your real Goddamn name. Not the name that bastard pastor gave you."

"Asenath," the girl screams.

Gene rips her off the couch by her hair, the girl shrieking, and he whips his empty beer at the wall, the bottle shattering against the picture of Lara on the horse, and the picture frame falls from the wall and cracks on the ground. A tuft of hair is entangled in his fingers and he blows it away with a breath, like a dandelion puff. The girl cowers at his feet, covering her head with her arms.

"Can't put a bird back in a nest," Gene slurs, grabbing the unopened beer and stumbling off to bed.

She is still there in the morning, watching him warily from her place on the couch. He is dressed for work, reeking of beer. "Come on then," he tells her, and she follows him out to his truck. They drive beyond the limits of Ulysses and get on US 191. It is Sunday, and the gates of the church are open, and the pastor's doves cluster along the road in their white gowns, young and old, men and women, greeting those who would attend service. Many doves wear the scars of their penance proudly. His focus picks among the brunette women although he knows she will not be there. Gene pulls the truck off to the side, across the street from the gathering. The girl sticks her head out the window like a hound sniffing at the air.

"They won't take you back," Gene says. "You know it. But I guess you got to do a thing to know it for real." He reaches across the girl and pops open her door. She hops down from the seat and limps across the road, white medical tape on her feet turning brown. A yellow sundress, one of Lara's, shows off her peeling shoulders. She doesn't look back. Gene gets going before witnessing an outcome that is never in doubt.

A month passes, time in which he returns to work, emergencies without end, the suffering of humans, the injury they do unto others and the injury they do unto themselves. A night run to Whiskey Cabaret, a couple of drunks brawling over nothing, one of the men split jaw to hairline with a broken bottle. Cops are there before the ambulance arrives, the drunk perpetrator spitting curses from the backseat of a squad car. Inside is smoke-filled, there's blood dripping from the bar, and the victim lies on his back tended to by the bartender, a white towel drenched red pressed to his face. Music plays overhead, what passes for modern country, and from behind a microphone a DJ announces the night's drink specials from a booth that overlooks an empty stage and a chrome stripper pole. The crowd, hard men who have yet to have the cowboy bred from their souls, keep to their drink with disinterest. Gene and his partner get to work, taking a look at the old fella's wound, the sour reek of liquor on the man's breath washing over them. They clean the cut and offer to transport the man, but he refuses, so they butterfly him up with some tape. The old man goes back to the bar and orders a drink.

It's as they are about to leave, the music shifts to a rock ballad, and the men at the bar are incited to hooting, migrating from their stools to fill the empty chairs circling the stage. From behind a curtain of glittery beads struts out a barefoot girl with dark hair and a landscape of old burn scars covering dimpled cheeks. A barely noticeable limp as she saunters across the stage, twirls around the pole in a tied off t-shirt that exposes the flawless skin of her midriff and the crater-pocked flesh of her shoulders. The DJ's voice announces, "Give it up men, for a former angel who traded in her wings to become a horny little devil, sweet, sexy—" The men around the stage wave their dollars as Gene bolts out the front door.

Outside, he looks up at the stars, more than he could ever count. He tries to catch his breath, overwhelmed, not by the innumerable constellations, but by all the black space between them. He walks over to the back of the ambulance and sits on the bumper. His partner follows him out and tries speaking with him, but Gene doesn't answer. He's untying his boots, stripping them off his feet, and peeling off his socks. The asphalt of the parking lot is warm on his soles, absorbing all the sun has to give during the day and parsing it out at night. Gene walks out to US 191 and faces east, plants his feet on the yellow dividing line, and takes his first step.

Gravity Haunted

M. Soledad Caballero

Before any flight our hearts beat hot, a furnace of red, blazing.
This, too, is prayer against the engines of the plane, against the
madness of a gravity that wins against reason and lifts the plane
while I close my eyes in wonder, petrified at the truth of science
and its tentacles. Beloved, we have lived this dance together for two
decades. You still tell me stories of Odysseus and his shipwrecked heart.
The way the gods always punish and also reward the traveler.
You whisper to me about battles of water and blood and half imagined
dreams, when whole ships plunged into the mouth of the ocean, when
Poseidon flung them across the dark mirror of the sea. Yes, you try, offer
me the stories of other bodies and other scars, as if they are a wish. But
when I think of flying, I imagine Penelope who knew travel cost her
all the love she had, all the men the Cyclops ate. And I remember
I have danced with gravity since I was a girl fleeing a dark, slender country.

PASSIVE-AGGRESSIVE FLOTSAM CROSS

HENRY GOLDKAMP

I was born.
A wet chunk of wood
clipped my shoulder,
kept charming me to sleep
with it. Gulp its mud. Why
shush such gravity? Strip
that semblance of gown
and pants. Let your animal
laugh. Reduce. Reuse. Recycle.
Earth chews fig leaves
with a mouth wide open.

I see me in the world.
Everything mirror, shard.

The eucharist is a fortune
cookie. *Do not speak
for others. Think for them.*
You must eat it. That's a rule.

The brute drools. The ark
sunk. Barnacles clot
heaven and its binnacle.

I will never see my heart.
Poor heart. Invisible blood
rubs invisible hearts awake.
A broiler of dark matter.

Dedicated menace.

O sack, bag, wrap, manila
envelope. Unhealthy to shed,
ungodly to witness.
                          Lamb
with human hands,
take a carpenter's hammer
to every pound of tooth.
Here I am, workbench
bewitched and rubber:
tongue, fingernails,
legs, nails. Lame hoof.

ORIGIN STORIES FOR THE TURTLE LADY

KENT KOSACK

You don't work in the toy business for forty-some-odd years without meeting a few colorful people. The mid–panic attack parents pounding on the door after you close on Christmas Eve; the heartbreaking kids wheeled in, frail and hairless from chemo, their eyes real glassy and deep in their skull. Once I was even held-up at knife point. There wasn't much money in the register and they caught the guy a week later robbing a convenience store, so maybe there's not much of a story there. But for a while after that I couldn't stock the rubber swords and plastic Rambo knives without sweating through my shirt.

Then there was the Turtle Lady. She had been a customer for a year before I started calling her that. A Top Toys regular with no time for small talk. One of those mothers on a mission making a beeline for the newest Teenage Mutant Ninja Turtle like it was the last case of water in a nation-wide drought. Sometimes she'd have the figure in her clutches before the string of bells on the front door stopped jingling.

She never bought other toys. Never even looked at any. Some mornings, when she was the first customer of the day, I swear she was a bird of prey, swooping through the store, passing the small-fry Teddy Ruxpins, the neon-bright Super Soakers, the stacks of yellow Play-Doh jars, the confounding Rubik's Cubes, aisle after aisle of flashy toys—she'd skip it all, flying straight to the Turtle corner and alighting on the newest Ninja Turtle without fail. She always seemed to know which iteration was most in demand. I figured either she did her research or her kid gave great instructions. Like, "This week, Mom, there's a version of Michelangelo as a football player. With shoulder pads and knee pads and a removable football that clicks into his hand. His arm actually throws. Like a real arm. A real arm!" My own kids used to sound like that. Back when they were kids and we used to talk. When they begged me to tell them stories and they listened, snug in their beds, their faces rapt-seeming even in sleep.

The hullabaloos around new toys are a boon for business. And on those busy, debut days, when parents were lined up outside before I opened, regardless of the weather, humming with anxiety, the dread of their child's disappointment looming behind them—on these days I'd keep one eye on the inventory and one looking out for our Turtle Lady. One such day I spied her in the crowd. She was easy to spot. Unlike the eager, indulgent look of the rest of the parents, her face was determined. Determined and miserable. I guessed because she was so torn up with worry that her kid wouldn't have the newest, coolest, most ingenious Teenage Mutant Ninja Turtle the day it was released. I thought she might have a stroke. I could imagine it. "Ma'am, we're sold out," I'd say, and she'd just look at me. Silent. Uncomprehending. I'd repeat myself two or three times to let it sink in and then all that maternal rage would float up into her brain like a blood clot and she'd keel over. No more foot soldiers to worry about. No more pizza to gorge on. No more sewers to patrol. The demise of the Turtle Lady.

Not that her obsession was so unique. A lot of parents came through like that, trapped with tunnel-vision for a certain toy. But the Turtle Lady seemed to operate at her own special frequency. Though I admired her doggedness, and appreciated the business, I secretly hoped she'd pick out another toy. Just once. Even if only to look at it. She never did. Never deviated from her schedule.

But back in 1990 I think, or maybe the end of '89, she stopped coming in. I didn't notice right away. Between the videogame store opening up at the mall and the release of the Gameboy, we were struggling to keep the store in the black. I lost a lot of sleep over how many units of Furbies to order and whether dollhouses could ever compete with Tetris. Days of soul-searching in the toy business. Confronting a lot of hard questions. But eventually I noticed her absence. Or one of my stock boys said something. And I guess I got curious. It felt like a bad omen for the store, losing such a steady and devoted customer, so I looked her up in our customer list.

Her name was Maria Bruno. She lived one town over in Midland Park. Which was weird, because they have their own toy store. A good one too. One of those family-run neighborhood establishments that feel permanent, a hearty part of the landscape like a big old oak. Popular enough that they often ran out of hot-selling toys, and sent customers over here, where toys took longer to sell out. Honestly, too long sometimes. But during a slow mid-week morning at the store, I got the idea to send her a card. I did this now and then, mostly to let loyal customers know when an exciting new toy was coming in and, yes, to remind them to come spend some of their money in my store. People liked it. And I liked sending them. The point was to be light, not nagging so much as thoughtful, funny even. Not another advertisement so much as your loyal and concerned toy seller checking in.

I wrote her full name and address on the postcard. The front had a nice glossy photo of the store all decked-out and lit-up for Christmas. On the back, I wrote:

> *Dear Mrs. Bruno (our Turtle Lady!),*
> *Your friends at Top Toys want to wish you well*
> *and let you know that the latest versions of your*
> *favorite mutated crime-fighting turtles have hit*
> *the shelves. Hope to see you soon. Cowabunga!*
> *—the Top Toys team*

Outside of the toy business, a grown man writing to a stranger about toys is weird. But I know my trade and people love that stuff. Or they used to anyway. I dropped it in a mailbox on my way home, confident that she'd appreciate the letter and the nickname. The kind of service you only get from a local store.

Nothing came of it for a month or so. The Turtle Lady remained in her shell. Until, on a bleak mid-March morning, she appeared, ready for her Turtle as if there'd never been a break in her routine. I remember she wasn't wearing a coat and her sweater had little beads of ice clinging to it, melting as I rang her up. I was proud of my postcard and couldn't resist breaching protocol and attempting some small talk with her.

"So, you're back. And with Mutagen Man. Good choice. He's a hit. For your son?" She looked at me and her mouth smiled but her eyes looked tired. "He's kind of a tragic character. Mutagen Man," I said.

I got no response other than the stiff smile so I plowed on, too quickly reading the back of the box as I waited for her receipt to print. The machine was on the fritz again, spitting out blank paper.

"He's five hundred pounds." I started to elaborate on the facts, looking at his guts through his clear plastic stomach. They were just floating there. All of his organs. Like things to be studied, soaked in formaldehyde. Some of these toys were on the morbid side. "He's a conflicted character. A villain, yes, but not your run-of-mill bad guy. No Bebop or Rocksteady. His body is breaking down. Look at his scaly skin. You can see the muscle poking through. And the eyes just suspended in the plastic blob of a body." I was getting carried away. It was a disturbing toy. "And he needs ooze to survive. He runs on the toxic stuff. That's why he helps Shredder. Only for the ooze." I looked up from futzing with the receipt printer and saw that the Turtle Lady was crying. Still wearing that weird half-smile, but bawling too. I didn't know what to do.

"Ma'am. I'm sorry. Would you like a tissue?" I thought about taking ten percent off but understood that it wouldn't help any.

She shook her head. I handed her the receipt. She took it, and Mutagen Man, and walked back into the sleet-coated world outside. The episode unnerved me. I couldn't read her and I pride myself on being able to read my customers. I went to the Turtle section and, to be doing something, reorganized the toys. I put the Turtles on the top along with the other good guys, their friends and sidekicks, mutant ducks and rats and rabbits. A reporter. An oddball in a hockey mask. Usually, I spread them out, intermixing allies and enemies. But I remember that day I banished the bad guys to the bottom row.

The Turtle Lady disappeared again. This time, I couldn't blame her. She came in to buy a toy for her kid and left in tears. Not exactly your typical toy-store experience. I felt terrible about it. I waited a month and decided to pay her a visit. I thought about sending another post-card or mailing her a special coupon but ended up thinking a face-to-face apology was the right thing to do. Sometimes all you can do is say you're sorry.

I drove over to Midland Park on a Monday. Our towns are so similar that if it weren't for a little blue sign welcoming you to Midland Park, you wouldn't know you ever left one place or were entering another. Her house was on the south end of town. A niceish neighborhood of two and three-bedroom Cape Cods and ranches, a mix of brick and vinyl-siding. Well-kept lawns but no lavish landscaping. Her house in the middle of the block was smaller and shabbier than I expected. Based on the number of Turtles she bought, I figured she had a decent amount of money. The house was a little dumpy and the yard too. It felt abandoned. The gloominess of the place made me reconsider my postcard plan. But I got out of the car after all and rang the doorbell—you have to have a certain amount of courage to make it in the toy business. It sounded a bit like a sleigh bell, only more muffled and flat. I had a new toy with me. A samurai panda. One of the Turtles' allies. I thought a cuter figure might cheer her up and help move the apology along. I'd used the same trick with my daughters, raiding the store for something to win them back after I'd disappointed them. A new doll, a skateboard. It worked, for a time. Worked until it didn't.

I rang the bell once more and the button got stuck. The bell kept ringing. In succession, it sounded like the sleigh had begun to move.

She came to the door with that same fixed smile. I said, "Hi. Hello. I'm the owner of Top Toys. We spoke about a month ago."

"I remember. Hello." She spoke softly but wasn't crying so I thought it was going well enough. Time to turn on the old toy sales- man charm, I thought.

"Yes. Well, I didn't get a chance to apologize before you left. You've been a loyal customer and of course I'm very sorry if I said anything that offended you. Very sorry." She didn't respond and I started to sweat. I could feel the dampness of my shirt matching the dampness of the green April day blooming behind me.

"And I brought Panda Khan here as part of my apology. He's a time-traveling, mutant, samurai bear." I held the figure out in front me, peace offering and shield. "Your son will love him."

She opened the door a bit wider and I saw what I should have guessed at much earlier—an armband wrapped around her upper- arm, a black mourning band thick enough almost to cover her arm from shoulder to elbow. I didn't notice in the store because she must have been wearing a dark sweater. Or I was too focused on the toy or the sleet melting in her hair or on feeding the cash register.

"Come in."

I went in and held the figure in its plastic box with both hands. I needed to hold onto something.

"Thank you for coming. It's kind."

The living room was full of drying flowers hanging upside down from a clothesline. I ducked under a bunch of inverted carnations and followed her down a carpeted hallway, not really sure of where we were heading until we came to a door with a large sticker on it the shape of a turtle shell.

"This is my son's room. You can leave it with the others in the corner if you'd like."

The room was small, shrunken. A big hospital bed stuck in the upright position blocked half of the only window in the room. The curtains were drawn. Along the opposite wall, a child's desk and chair. A lamp with what looked like crayon wax melted along the bottom. A narrow closet. Very little else other than, in one corner, the son's collection, all the Turtles she'd ever bought, piled high like a plastic pyre. I put the panda on top. The toys seemed, suddenly, like what they were: cheap, mass-produced plastic figurines. And I? The lonely man peddling them.

"I'm very sorry for your loss," I said.

"He always wanted to come to your store, you know. But I never let him. I liked the surprise on his face when he saw the new Turtle on our front steps. I'd set them outside just before his bus dropped him off." She nodded towards the mound of plastic figures. "It didn't matter which. I'd go out front and watch him through the window. He'd play with them but they'd never fight. He'd just have them tell each other stories. Make introductions. He would memorize the blurbs on the boxes and then add to them. Long stories about their homeland, their families, their hopes for the future." She smiled then, and her eyes smiled too. "Like a tea party, I guess."

"I'm very sorry. I didn't know," I said, thinking of my daughters at that age. Their miniature furniture and tea sets. The stories we'd create together. As kids they could imagine anything, whole worlds, alternate realities.

"When he got too sick to go to school, I lined them up on the end of his bed. Like they just arrived to visit him." Her smile tightened. "I don't need them now. I bought the last one out of habit. I missed the feeling of coming home with something for him. Of coming home to him."

There they were, all of them. The core group. The original toys. Then, the larger family of accomplices and allies, of rivals and villains. The multiple versions of each Turtle: The detective Turtle in a trench coat. The slice-and-dice Turtle with the moving arms. A lumpish villain that was a disembodied and tentacled brain. I thought of all those hours in the toy store, hours I spent reading the stories on their boxes. The figures were dead and dull in their packaging, despite the articulated joints and bright costumes and elaborate backstories, without a child's imagination to animate them.

"They are amazing, aren't they?"

I said they were.

"Do you want them? I was thinking of donating them. Or maybe keeping a few." She bent down and picked up one. "He liked this gold robot, I think."

"That's the Fugitoid," I said, the names ingrained from hours of stocking shelves.

"The Fugitoid," she said, moving the odd word around her mouth as she moved the robot's arms and legs.

"He helps the Turtles. He was a doctor originally." I picked up another. "And of course, you know Splinter?"

She shook her head. Her eyes were focused on Splinter. Really focused. I don't think she saw me at all. I sat down next to the pile, cross-legged like a little kid. From the floor, the room didn't seem so small. I thought of all those parents lining up in front of my store and I felt sorry that neither I nor Maria Bruno would ever again be among them.

"Well, let me give you some background on him. There's so much to tell," I said, digging into the pile. I heard her sob. Loud, like some sort of congestion in her chest breaking up and apart. But she kept listening. I kept talking. Neither of us could stop.

STUDIES IN EROSION

KRISTEN HOLT-BROWNING

It had been a time of erosion. I'd begun to see in metaphor.
(Dani Shapiro, *Hourglass)*

I.

The funeral director handed me a heavy cardboard box. Heavy only because I expected lightness. A life reduced to flaky dust: a heavy knowledge. My father.

I dug a hole beneath the lilac bush I had planted two years earlier. It was struggling: green all season, but it never blossomed all that much. I scattered the ash in the soil beneath the plant. Would this kill it? I didn't know, I didn't want to follow the twisted paths of the internet this query would lead me down. I dug a hole and tipped the ashes in. The lilac did not die, but it still didn't flourish.

Four years later, we moved to a big, shiny new house across town. I still drive by our first house sometimes, my two kids strapped down in the backseat. The new residents put up a fence, so I can't see the lilac, don't know if it's still there, if it died. One-third of my father in a yard of strangers, who never see, never know, what's beneath their dirt.

II.

The creekside beach has gone vertical. Once a gentle slope, it has been worn at its base by the ever-passing water. The reservoir upstream is regularly released; the surge of tide has scraped the beach out from beneath itself, and now it's a steep hill. Ropes run its length. You heave yourself up the slope, dripping wet and sand-encrusted.

I never liked this snake-filled place. The water murky, the swim instructors insistent that you jump into the deep end off the dock, that this would somehow teach an eight-year-old the mechanics of moving arms and legs to stay afloat.

I haven't been back in more than twenty years, when I was just swimming out of adolescence, grasping at those shiny-sharp crags of adulthood. I didn't need this dinky creek, this crumbly beach, this tired non-town. I was big-city, I was metaphor, I was the oldest story in the book. My father was alive.

I am forty-two, and my ten-year-old son is jumping off the dock. Time has eroded my boy's soft baby places into sharper angles, bonier elbows and knees. I look down on him and watch his cannonball body slice the air above the water in the second before he goes under.

"Was it always this steep?" I ask my best friend, standing next to me with her toddler perched on her hip.

"No," she tells me. "It keeps getting worse."

III.

Some words, at some times, bear the additional weight of meaning beyond meaning. For months now, this word—*erosion*—has been jammed in my mind, stuck against a hard rock in my subconscious.

It's a beautiful word. It's a gentle degradation. But is it too pretty? Hard bone ground to ash. A shoreline impossible to scale.

> *I would not want, I think, a higher intelligence, one*
> *simultaneous, cut clean*
> *of sequence.*
>
> (Jorie Graham, "Erosion")

I interpret this divine horror as: no movement, so no decay. No breaking down. But then no rising up. My father alive and dead. My son a baby and not. My little human mind nauseous as time bucks and falters. My body not built to house such higher intelligence, if that's what it is. It feels more like a flattening, a ravaging.

In that same poem, Graham writes about "trying to feel the

erosion." This I understand. I, too, want to place my hand on rock and feel the crumbling, the invisible, the inevitable. If I can hold the body decaying, the baby aging, the ground wearing down beneath my feet—then, what? I want to imagine there's a power in this knowledge: You're not fooling me. I know what's happening.

Maybe this is all the arc of time bends toward: ashes forever disappearing in the breeze. Sand shifting and roiling beneath feet.

At this point, I will cling to any metaphor that will have me. Even if it crumbles in my palm. Even if all that remains is the single shard of bone in the ash. That rock forcing the water to part around it. Always losing infinitesimal parts of itself. All of this is metaphor. All of this is true.

Hydrangea

Rachel Hinton

In your next paycheck there will be one
thousand more dollars, this is one of the
many ways, your boss says, they will show
great esteem, and esteem is a word pushed forward like
spring, like hydrangea. What are the
proper reasons for elation? One thousand is one
portion of what you make, you
make fifty though what you make should not make it out
you are elated and petaled and
you are a puff of hydrangea flying, a token of great esteem.
You want to talk to your dad so you go to a website,
buy a floral top and a striped top, it is the time for
spring in your mind. Your boyfriend said you never
buy anything for yourself and you are high, buying.
You wish to be emergent, planetary, a conduit for the coming
big disaster but first you just need to
do this one quick thing.
Pour out, as your inbox fills with warnings of
capsize and Softest Tees Ever We Just Got an
Extension and the Climate Won't Wait, these are all
emails of happiness. Each is a
work, each pushes its little lozenge of
work to the world. Its excellent life, you are
possible to you, are changing. You cannot

talk to your dad, he was the
highjump champion of the Lake Wales schools and
you are the champion of
having a thousand dollars, it
is a thousand lakes to be the flowers beckoning over,
it is one fiftieth of what you make (you should not be candid about
what you make O to demur in your beckoning to be shy and not
dead about dollars). How much does it take?
You can den in offices far from your dead.
They are not skimming toward you on roads anymore,
you don't have a car even
to be hovering in fear over—
you divested yourself of it years ago, plunked it
in active breakdown. Around it
oniony greens shot up. It was
spring, valleying you in tenderness,
opening its drenched mouth.

Song of the South, Reprise

Sean Enfield

I have this recurring dream—call it a fantasy if you want—in which I travel back in time to 1940s rural Mississippi and tell my white grandma that I'm her future black grandson. We call her Memaw, but she'd have been Irma then. She wouldn't have the wrinkled, sun-splotched skin or the short, wavy white hair we know her by now but would be the country girl wearing the long plaid skirts in the old black-and-white photographs she used to send me.

I picture it like this ...

She faints almost immediately, confused both by the marvel of time travel and the horror of the brown-skinned young man proclaiming himself her kin. I picture us by a creek, because all of her childhood stories seem to take place by a creek, or maybe they don't and maybe I just picture the Mississippi of Memaw's youth as a network of creeks and streams, weaving around ghost towns. After she tips over, I find a seat on a nearby log and wait for her to come to. I want to talk, about what I'm not sure. Mainly, I want to see if she'd love me without having given birth to the son that I call Dad. I want to see if she could even conceive of loving me at that time in her life—growing up in the Deep South and attending a whites-only school—at a time when her favorite movie was *Song of the South*, the long forgotten Disney film in which a docile, servile Negro tells happy stories and sings happy songs and makes the movie's white children, well, happy.

In the commotion, however, Memaw's brothers[1] come running from the house up the hill, and being from the future, I'd know this scene from history books. The young black man hovering over the incapacitated young white girl can only mean one thing, and so I start clicking my heels, "There's no place like home, there's no place like home," or hop in the DeLorean or however I travelled through time. The conversation, even in my dreams, still goes unspoken; once again, I'm left wondering if it's only the blood in my veins, proof of a lineage, that compels Memaw to love me even as it runs beneath a skin tone I know frightens her.

Released first in 1946, and re-released in the '70s and ' 80s, Disney's *Song of the South* once had a reputation as a landmark film, though it has since been spurned and locked away deep, deep, deep in Disney's hallowed vault. Its song, "Zip-a-Dee-Do-Dah," won the Academy Award for Best Original song and can still be heard while rushing down the waters of Splash Mountain, which also features characters from the movie, in Disney World's Magic Kingdom. Though initially a commercial disappointment, in part due to its regressive racial depictions, the film eventually earned Disney quite a bit of money during its 1972, 1980, and 1986 theatrical reissues, and until 2009's *The Princess and the Frog*, no other Disney theatrical film featured a black character in a lead role besides *Song of the South*. [2]

Still, the movie is mostly known as one of those notoriously racist films of yesteryear, like *Birth of a Nation* before it, the blemish on a Hollywood with a face like a pubescent teenager. As such, *Song of the South* has never seen a release on either VHS or DVD and hasn't been screened since its fortieth anniversary in 1986, though there are those who advocate for the movie's re-release—out of morbid curiosity, maybe, nostalgia, certainly, but mostly because they see some value in the movie and its depiction of race. [3]

---

[1] I've never met any of Memaw's immediate family, most having died before my own consciousness, but in the photos she'd send, they all looked like the stoic, strong-chinned men from Civil War photos, staring into some distance I'd never see. Of course, these photos would've been taken more than eighty years after the Civil War.

[2] Jason Sperb. *Disney's Most Notorious Film: Race, Convergence, and the Hidden Histories of Song of the South*, University of Texas Press, 2012.

[3] Christian Willis is one such fan of the movie. Since 1999, he has maintained the domain, songofthesouth.net, to keep an online repository for all things *Song of the South* as a testament to all things past, present and future about a movie infamously associated with the past because, in his words, "*Song of the South* will always have a future to be recorded, and I'll be keeping track of it!"

Somehow, however, Memaw possessed a bootlegged copy of the movie on a beat up old VHS tape, and one summer, trapped in her Arizona home in a little city outside of Phoenix, she presented it to my sisters and I as some sort of marvel, a cultural relic which, I suppose, it was.

"This was one of my favorite movies growing up," she told us.

This was in 2004, eighteen years after the movie had last been given a proper release. I was twelve and my sisters were eleven, and already we were forgetting about the medium of VHS tapes, our parents having donated all of ours in favor of a growing DVD collection at our house back home in Texas. On the front of the tape, the title, *Song of the South*, was scrawled on a white sticker with a big, fat black marker and gave it even more the appearance of some strange, forgotten artifact.

We were used to Memaw showing us old movies she loved—*The Secret Garden, Anne of Green Gables*, and a whole bunch of movies starring Shirley Temple. Arizona summers are unbearably hot, and aside from swim team practices and swim meets, we spent most of our summers visiting Memaw and Pepaw indoors, watching TV and playing video games. Every now and then, Memaw would walk into the living room, horrified by whatever cartoon[4] we were watching, and pull a tape out for us to watch instead.

"Here," she would say, "this is much better."

Out of all those movies, however, *Song of the South* stood out as being particularly removed from a time and place we recognized. The movie, based on black folklore written by a white man, Joel Chandler Harris[5], takes place on a Georgia plantation, set in a South that is somehow simultaneously pre-and post-Civil War. Johnny and his parents move to this magical plantation where the help looks and acts like slaves but are never once called slaves. While there, the young Johnny befriends the kindly old Uncle Remus[6], who could just as easily be named Uncle Tom. Uncle Remus is the picture-perfect

---

[4] She particularly hated Spongebob Squarepants.

[5] A writer for various local newspapers in Georgia from 1862-1900 whose collection, "Uncle Remus: His Songs and Sayings," based on his interactions with and the folklore gleaned from black slaves on the Turnwold Plantation, was adapted into *Song of South*.

[6] Portrayed by New York actor, James Baskett, who could not, due to segregation laws, attend the movie's Atlanta premiere but later won a "special Oscar" for his "able and heart-warming characterization of Uncle Remus" two years after its release.

definition of the Magic Negro archetype, imbued both with an otherworldly wisdom and a self-effacing humility, that allows him to regale Johnny with tales of Br'er Rabbit and Br'er Fox and Br'er Bear and Br'er Frog, all while a cartoon Mr. Bluebird whistles away on his shoulder. In what was cutting edge at the time, the movie blends live action performance and animation—Uncle Remus and Johnny inhabiting the world of reality whereas the cartoon critters from Remus' tales are rendered in a deliriously delightful animation.

The movie presents a racial harmony that seems as if it should've appealed to three mixed-race children, but being mixed, we'd already begun to find that harmony suspect. Being mixed isn't to see the world in some marvelous, harmonious shade of gray, like the two races that give your skin that natural and oft-desirable tan. Being mixed, instead, is to see everything in a stark black-and-white, except for yourself who hangs perilously from the line of division. So even then, before I knew much about the condition of my skin, I watched the movie confused by its sing-along depiction of a plantation. I didn't yet have the language to classify this confusion, only a feeling that something was awry about Memaw's singsong version of history. I saw with "double consciousness," though I wouldn't encounter DuBois's term for at least another decade.

Song of the South reminded me of *Gone with the Wind*, another movie Memaw had put on for us, but this time with cartoon musical numbers instead of death and miscarriages. Nonetheless, blackness occupied such a horrifying and yet cheerful space in both movies—the happy-go-lucky slave in *Gone with the Wind*'s periphery is foregrounded in Disney's film and even given songs to sing. I knew the movie, and all its uplifting music, wanted me to feel warm, but glancing down at my brown skin, I never felt more cold and alien. As the film neared its end, Memaw hummed along to its most famous of songs, "Zip-a-Dee-Do-Dah," while Uncle Remus, Johnny, and the cartoon critters sang us into the credits, "My, oh my, what a wonderful day."

"Don't you just love it?" she asked us, beaming as she removed the tape from the VHS player, and we nodded yes, unsure if we were allowed to answer any other way.

I didn't intend to write about Memaw, only about that curious tape of hers. In fact, not until a decade after we had watched the movie did I realize how scandalous it was that she even had that tape and that she screened it for us, her black grandchildren. I was listening to a comedy podcast and the host made an offhand remark about a movie locked forever in the Disney vault, *Song of the South*, and that part of my brain where I stored all of Memaw's peculiarities lit up and started flashing and gave way to the obsessive, research-oriented part of me I was then indulging in my studies at the University of North Texas.

Article after article returned me to that Arizona living room and provided names for the strange feelings that overcame me as I sat watching the kindly, old black man sing songs of joy to and with his oppressors. And the more I read, the more I realized how peculiar it was that I had even seen this movie at all and that it had been presented to me, not as a relic of racism past, but as a darling part of Memaw's childhood, something to cherish even though the studio that made it had tried to bury it six years before my birth. I felt angry, but what angered me seemed so absurd that it felt useless to try and make sense of any of it, so I let it hang over me instead, like some cosmic void to which I might credit my existence.

In that entanglement of absurdity and anger I see Memaw who loved us, her black grandchildren, and who loved *Song of the South*, the Disney movie that horrified us. In college, I'd learn from my mother that Memaw ignored the fact of my father's marrying a black woman for two years. She wouldn't mention my mother at all to any family member who hadn't received a wedding invite. Sometimes, I wonder how my mother wore those two years, a literal black sheep. Did she doubt the love my father felt because of the hate from the woman who made him? Probably she tried to block it out, the way Memaw had tried to block her out. I suppose Memaw hoped my father's jungle fever would pass, but once it bore fruit, she had no choice but accept the relationship as something more than a phase. There was a grandson now whose skin was forever evidence of the transgression, and she became the good, Christian grandmother I presumed she envisioned herself to be.

Those summers in her house were like church camps only my sisters and I attended. She taught us to cook, drove us to our swimming lessons and swim meets, and enrolled us in week-long Sunday school classes called Vacation Bible School. Worried our mother was letting us get too fat, she would hide artificial sweeteners in our Kool-Aid, and then say, grinning, "You couldn't even tell," as we struggled to sip our cups empty. That was Memaw for us, a glass of Kool-Aid made bitter.

I didn't intend to write about Memaw because I never thought I would or could write about her. Maybe, after she passed, I could hide her likeness in a work of fiction—some kooky old lady ranting to her colored daughter-in-law and grandchildren about the new "colored" folks who moved into her neighborhood. Even then, I think I would refute any family member who tried to say that, hey, that's exactly what Memaw did! Its fiction, I'd insist, completely fabricated. Some things work better when you frame them as fictional, true though they may be.

And yet, here I am, writing about her by the name she prefers, Memaw, because she thought grandma sounded *too old*.

During my undergraduate studies, she would call me often, tell me stories from her childhood, apologize for taking up so much of my time, suggest she should hang up, and then tell me more stories from her childhood. She almost always ended the calls by reminding me that I was a writer. "One day," she'd say, "you might be able to use my stories." And the words, though always framed as a suggestion, had the charge of a command. *You will tell my story, grandson.*

Showing us *Song of the South* was preparation for these stories. The issue of race likely never occurred to her, as it never occurred to her that children could tell the difference between artificial and real sugars. She wanted to give us a glimpse into a past as she viewed it, but her nostalgia didn't line up with the history.

Her stories became more and more urgent as she got older. After a brief skin cancer scare that ended up benign, she framed almost every conversation as potentially one of her last, despite her otherwise clean bill of health. I guess this is something we do as we age. Eventually, our every conversation circles back to our eventual deaths, and we want to make sure someone remembers us, even those like her who lived devout Christian lives and believed that Jesus knew her name in life and would in death, too. For Memaw, this shift occurred in her seventies. And so the line, "You might be able to use my stories someday," grew an ugly, morbid appendage, "Hopefully, I'll be around to read them!" Her Christmas letters and birthday cards, too, became filled with her childhood stories, and with pictures of her and her family, sometimes copies and sometimes the original print. I kept them for a time, a possibility.

She called again in 2012, my first presidential election. I paced around the yard outside my apartment while she tried to convince me not to vote for Barack Obama. I hadn't, at any point in the conversation or in any of our conversations, told her that I planned to vote for Obama; I knew better than that, and yet she felt compelled to make sure I made "the right vote." She had made the same call to my mother four years prior. "I know you're black," she began, "but you can't vote for that Obama." For me, however, she simply began, "That Barack is the Antichrist." The rest of her argument followed suit, typical right-wing conspiracy theories—Barack was a secret Muslim, wasn't an American citizen, was a socialist. She said nothing about his policies, his imperialist strategies overseas, his massive deportations of which I suspected she might've approved, and she never mentioned his, or my, race. Still, I couldn't help but see Obama's light-skin and, by extension my own, as she talked. I stared into the sun and wished she would switch into one of those Mississippi stories or something. As usual, however, I simply listened and clenched my fist all the while.

I've never wanted to write about Memaw because I knew I couldn't do it the way she wanted me to. If I ever started her story, I'd hear the old woman who called to warn me about the villainous black man who wanted to destroy America. I'd hear the old woman who, as we sat in her living room watching news reports on the aftermath of Hurricane Katrina, proclaimed aloud, "Finally God is punishing those people for living in sin," as the TV showed black bodies crying over their broken homes. I'd hear the old woman who warned me to steer clear of Mexicans, who couldn't distinguish between immigrants and invaders, and who warned my sisters not to marry a Muslim man minutes after they'd graduated college. I'd hear her call the first black president *The Anti-Christ*, and the story would never take shape. Always, I nodded along, silently, suppressing the anger and confusion mounting within. I can't see the young woman in her stories, who sang "Zip-a-Dee-Doo-Dah" while she fished with her brothers, not through the bitter, ignorant, and sometimes hateful old woman she'd become, and I struggle to see the kind, Christian woman she perceives herself to be.

"He's the Antichrist, I tell you," she concluded, "Romney, on the other hand, is a fine Christian man."

"Yes, Memaw," I said, "I've gotta go. Love you."

I couldn't write her story. After that call, I took those old letters, those old photographs, and all the memories that they contained, and I tossed them in the trash, and I pulled some old, rotten leftovers from the fridge, and as those stern, white faces peered up to from the trash and from decades ago, I dumped the stinking food over top, hitting the bottom of the plastic container so that every drop of mildewed juice drizzled into the bin, in case I got the urge to undo what I should've done some time ago.

What do we do with a history we'd rather forget? And what if that history is your ancestry, an irremovable part of the lineage that made you? Are we justified to lock it in a vault as Disney has done, never to be seen again? I do not challenge Memaw's hate, and I can't say if the inaction is a result of love or fear or some curious blending of the two. When she warns me of "Mexican cartel members smuggling drugs in the diapers of babies crossing the border," I nod and change the subject. Perhaps, it's learned behavior—conditioned from summers at her side mouthing along to Baptist hymnals that seemed to me antiquated and false. Always, I assume the role of dutiful grandson in her presence.

The first summer we spent with her, when I was eleven, I bowed my head when the pastor visiting her church said so. I could feel the light coming in from the pulpit. "Would anyone here like to know the loving grace of Jesus?" the pastor asked the whole congregation. "Then raise your hand. The Lord sees you."

Memaw patted my back when he instructed the unsaved to raise their hands, knowing we'd yet to be baptized, and I know what she expected of me, and so as I would do time and time again afterwards, I shrunk myself on her behalf. I raised my hand dutifully and would be baptized that summer.

And when she calls, more than a decade later, to see if I've found a church in Fairbanks, Alaska, where I'm working toward my Master's in creative writing, I tell her, "Yes, a Baptist one too." And when she asks that I pray for our president, the man supported by white nationalists and the Ku Klux Klan alike, I tell her, "Of course, I do every night," which isn't a lie technically, though our prayers take on different forms. She prays God's wisdom for him as he "makes America great again," and I pray for him and all those red hats make a swift exit from the political stage and into the Disney vault, a curious relic of history.

But maybe it's better to face these demons head on. There's no reconciling with the monster concealed behind concrete walls, only a perpetual terror that it might one day (that it will one day) reveal its ugly head again. In the post-1945 Germany, there is a word, *Vergangenheitsbewältigung*, which translates to "coping with the past," that has become a key concept in the discourse around German culture in the aftermath of the Holocaust. Another translation reads "a public debate within a country on a problematic period of its recent history." We have no such word for our many moral failings, for our troubled history. In the absence, we have a silence that demands nothing of us, a quiet concession to the grandmothers that supposedly have the best interests of our souls in mind in spite of the soil of our skin. We must cope with our Holocaust or else, as Baldwin warned, fulfill the prophecy, "*No more water, the fire next time.*" No future can emerge from a nostalgic past, from an America ever considered "great," only a ceaseless and consumptive burning.

I've seen firsthand the devastation of the fire from Baldwin's vision. I've born witness to a small, powerful glimpse of a Germany that hasn't coped with the past. I've met a Holocaust denier, and I observed in her a pattern not unlike that which governs my grandmother's own ignorance. Her name was Helga, and she was an old German woman, either in her seventies or eighties, who moved to the United States pre-reunification of Germany. She attended our family's church, the little storefront church we started going to shortly after the summer I got "saved." After a sermon in which the pastor quoted psychiatrist and Holocaust survivor, Viktor Frankl, she proclaimed loudly in the church lobby, "That man"—referring to Frankl—"is a liar. He wants only to besmirch our great Germany."

The Frankl quote had been a harmless one, a bit of inspirational wisdom elevated by the knowledge of its speaker's past sufferings, "If you're alive, you can find something beautiful in the world," and yet Helga needed to refute it, Frankl's very existence a threat to her vision of a great Germany that never was. I don't know much about Helga—why she left Germany for the US, how she arrived at her denial. She came to church sporadically, brought by a younger relative, presumably a granddaughter, who seldom spoke to any of the other congregation members. Helga herself usually sat quietly in the back row and nodded with a spurious smile whenever spoken to. I had never heard her string together more words than when she chose to denounce Frankl, and I never would again, even though she continued her sporadic attendance.

I know that she would've been a young girl in in Nazi Germany just as Memaw was a young girl in the Jim Crow South, and I know that she needed Frankl, and all other Holocaust survivors, to assume a villainous role in order to preserve an idyllic Germany that never was. When Memaw proclaims Obama the Antichrist, she might as well deny the fact of slavery, the fact of segregation, the fact of black mass incarceration, as Helga denies the fact of the Holocaust in calling Frankl a liar. To accept the significance of a black president is to accept an America that has long profited off the subjugation of black bodies and is to ruin the history she thought she knew, the story she'd like her grandson to write.

I've let most of Memaw's stories slip from my mind. I can tell you that race doesn't factor into them. They are nebulous affairs, harmless gallivanting about the Mississippi delta and the trouble that ensues. In this regard, they aren't much different than Uncle Remus's Br'er Rabbit tales. Br'er Rabbit attempts to run away from home. Br'er Rabbit outsmarts Br'er Fox with the "Tar Baby." Br'er Rabbit goes to his "laughing place." Fun stories meant to charm and entertain and teach and placate the young, white boy, and in them everyone is happy and all is well and no one hurts when they've ended. There's a reason she loves *Song of the South*, why it's resonated with her across decades and why she chose to show it to us that summer, and it's right there in the title song:

> I seem to hear those gentle
> voices calling low
> Out of the long long ago
> This heart of mine is in the heart of Dixie
> That's where I belong
> Singing a song, a Song of the South. [7]

She needs these stories; she needs them to bring her back to a south she remembers not as a story, in fact—because stories require conflict, complexity—but as a simple song. As such, she needs to ignore that they are told on a plantation and by black man, a servant of the seven year old boy to whom he tells them. She needs to discredit and dehumanize anything that threatens the validity and the purity of those stories. She wants only those "gentle voices" from the "long long ago," mystical, fantastical voice; whereas, I hear the low singing of slaves in the song of the South, not to pass the time but to mask an anguish—the voices that say, when she insists America was once as great as "Song of the South" suggests, *but c'mon … what about the "Tar Baby" though?*

Whether you've seen *Song of the South* or not, and more than likely you have not, you may have heard its pivotal song, "Zip-a-Dee-Doo-Dah," a song that feels like a precursor to *The Lion King*'s "Hakuna Matata" in its sheer, unwavering pleasantry and everything-is-going-to-be-all-right ethos. I had even heard it prior to having seen the movie. When I was around ten years old, Memaw and Pepaw paid for the whole family—themselves, my parents, my sisters, and I—to go to Disneyland, and there we rode Splash Mountain. The characters—Br'er Rabbit, Br'er Fox, Br'er Frog, and the like[8] —are goofy cartoon animals that greet us with smiles as we approach the ride proper. We don't recognize them from the pantheon of Disney films, having not ye yet seen the movie, and so they seem innocuous, invented for the solely for the ride. In fact, Br'er Rabbit and his ilk barely register to

---

[7] Sam Coslow. "Song of the South." *Song of the South*. Walt Disney Productions, 1946.
[8] Thankfully, the Tar Baby doesn't make an appearance.

us, especially after the excitement of taking a photos with Mickey Mouse and Buzz Lightyear on the walk up.

On Splash Mountain, a log flume pulls you through a cozy, Southern scene. Animatronic critters engage in all manners of goofy shenanigans, and eventually the flume descends into a slow exit back into daylight. As the ride ends, you come upon Br'er Rabbit, leaning casually against a tree trunk, whistling "Zip-a-Dee-Doo-Dah" to himself and to the passersby. The melody is so overwhelmingly jubilant that, once heard, you'll hum it for the remainder of the trip, even as Memaw complains constantly about your mom's, her daughter-in-law's, supposed laziness on display. The humming is eventually deployed in an attempt to tune out the growing dissention. *This is supposed to the happiest place on earth*, the humming insists, *so why is Mom insisting that she'd rather walk back to Texas than endure another moment with Memaw?*

In his "Humble Defense" of the film, first published online in 1999[9], Christian Willis writes[10],

> At least *Song of the South* made an attempt at showing harmony. And not only did it attempt at showing harmony within a family, but harmony between races as well; I think that's a big accomplishment for a film made in the 1940's when segregation was, sadly, still very much a part of life.

That harmony in the face of abject division and subjugation, more than anything, is what irks me about this movie and my grandmother's love of it, and it is that harmony, the Zip-a-Dee-Doo-Dah attitude, that leads me to believe that we are right to leave this movie locked away in Disney's vault. The movie has never seen a home release, on VHS or on DVD and not now on any streaming platform; I do not know how Memaw happened upon a tape, though it must've been hard to obtain, but having seen the movie, I say leave it in the cellar where it belongs. Let it drift away to a space outside of memory.

---

9 The stated purpose of Willis' website is to "provide the public with the most information possible on *Song of the South*," though it functions primarily as a testament to why the film should be re-released in some capacity, Willis being an admitted fan of the movie.

10 Christian Willis. "In Humble Defense," SongoftheSouth.net, 30 July 2008, http://www.songofthesouth.net/movie/overview/defense.html

To watch this movie isn't to grapple with a real and present racism, to struggle with the horror palpable in the fact of American slavery, or to contend with the segregated society into which the movie entered. No, watching the movie only perpetuates the silence that sustains the othering required to preserve the "American Dream," the song of the South. It opens up no conversation; rather, it closes any and all discourse with the delight of nostalgia.

The movie is a falsehood. In this regard, it is no different than those goofy red "Make America Great Again" hats, or the confederate statues the hat wearers want to preserve. Like the statues, most of which were erected by the Daughters of the Confederacy during the Civil Rights Era, *Song of the South* didn't emerge from the period it depicts but from white fear of black advancement. The movie saw its re-releases in the '70s and '80s to comfort a white populace still reeling from the movements of the decades prior, and to terrorize a black populace who had forgotten its place. Its nostalgic, or in Willis's words, "harmonious," depiction of the South lends itself to the lie that America has dealt with its past, that we've confronted our grandmothers and grandfathers, that we've coped with their violence. To watch the movie is to walk through "The Happiest Place on Earth," humming a ditty while your grandmother bombards your mom with racial stereotypes to the point that your mom starts looking up flights back to Texas days before the trip is supposed to end. It doesn't suggest that racial divisions can be healed; it suggests there's no rift at all and that there never has been. If Uncle Remus can sing, "Plenty of sunshine headin' my way," as he waltzes over the black blood in the Georgian soil, then the wound hasn't healed or scarred but has, instead, been scabbed over and picked at with a fingernail. It bleeds as he whistles, and I recoil in horror at the so-called harmony.

In that recurring dream of mine, I have never once had a conversation with Memaw, never once gotten to tell her that I'll be her grandson, because to do so would give way to the same Technicolor fantasy in *Song of the South* that dismays me. Whether in reality or in dream, I do not exist in that time of her life, and she would never love me then, could never be made to love me then. The history remains and always will remain as it was. No use trying to change it. Instead, we can engage it for what it was, is, and will mean for our future. Neither I nor my mom have confronted Memaw when she calls into question our black skin or the black skin of others, but have instead suffered the same silence.

Still, I'd like to believe there's some part of her, even through all the bitterness and hate, that could see past the nostalgia for the horrifying reality it masks. Maybe that's the part of her that loves us, her black grandchildren, but I don't know what reconciliation Memaw has made with our black skin or if she's reconciled with it at all. I suspect she has whistled it away, pretended it doesn't exist, proclaimed that it doesn't matter, and yet I have a new fantasy—call it a reoccurring dream—in which we, she and I, cope with our past and come to love each other not in spite of that great and heavy history, but with an awareness of it that lodges its way into memory like a melody you cannot shake.

Grandma's Letters

Paige Wallace
Ooligan Press 2019 Write to Publish winner

Our correspondence began when I went to college. I remember my campus mailbox, a tiny aged steel door tucked into a wall. The little key that opened it, crunching metal gears as it cranked the lock. Hundreds of mailboxes on that wall, but only one held a letter from my grandmother.

She always used pretty stationery. Often a pale green, her favorite color, with sweet pea blossoms vining around softly scalloped edges.

She always wrote in the room she called her den. I remember sitting with her at the thick oak table as she crafted letters to friends and relatives. My little girl legs swung wildly below my chair, too short to reach the ground. My chubby arms stretched above my chest to reach the tabletop. Grandma's handwriting swirled and looped, a perfect example of the penmanship a proper young lady learns inside a one-room schoolhouse on the Nebraska prairie. I would "write" along with her, colorful crayon curls on an oversized pad of scratch paper.

Her letters told me the stories of her life. Stories of her neighbors and relatives, courtships and deaths, plantings and harvests. Church picnics and dances at the Elks Lodge. The floats she saw in our hometown's Strawberry Festival Parade. Which of her beloved flowers were blooming, and what kind of pie she made yesterday.

She also sometimes wrote about the memories she carried with her from her past. The time Grandpa drove his new Model T Ford through a gate because he tried to stop it by yelling, "Whoa!" Memories of the baby they lost, their first child, because antibiotics did not exist yet—at least not for people who lived miles from a doctor, on a rural ranch, with little money.

Grandma also wrote to me when I lived in a small apartment with a boyfriend I thought I would marry. One morning, he woke me before my alarm.

"You're going to have a busy day at work."

"Why?" I asked, still groggy. I briefly considered my job as a news copywriter, then rolled over to get some more sleep.

"A plane just crashed into the World Trade Center."

By the time I had showered, the second plane had hit. It was, indeed, a busy workday, and a strange time. Like so many of us who lived through 9/11, I began to think about the fragility of life, the uncertainty of tomorrow. About the people we love.

The following Sunday, I wrote to Grandma. I told her about the wedding I had attended that weekend, four days after the attack. How the couple considered canceling, but ultimately decided they needed to go through with it. How the groom asked local friends to stand in at the last minute, because his groomsmen from the East Coast could not get here, with planes grounded. How the caterer drove up to the reception in his food truck, with the words "Bomb the Bastards" blasted in spray paint across the cart's metal siding. How it felt good to celebrate love in the wake of so much hatred.

She wrote back, right away. We began exchanging letters more intentionally and more often.

In one letter the following summer, I mentioned how much I hated the Fourth of July. Fireworks exploded right outside my second-story apartment window all night. My cat cowered underneath the bed. I felt like doing the same. Grandma wrote back that she, too, disliked the holiday. She said she once watched a little girl lose her hand in a fireworks blast, back in the day when explosive devices could be sold without warnings or legal limitations. This is not the kind of thing she would ever tell me in person. It was too graphic, maybe, or too sad. Written words made some stories possible.

When my relationship with the boyfriend ended, I took solace in my grandmother's letters, in her reassurance that I would find the right person someday. I read her words, sitting alone in that second-story apartment, and tried to believe. I always trusted the stories she shared with me. Perhaps I could trust this, too.

What I loved most about her letters was that each one began with the same salutation: "Dear Paigey Girl." No one ever called me that, except Grandma and Grandpa. It's a nickname I will never hear spoken again. After seventy-seven years of marriage, they died within a month of each other.

Years later, as my childhood home was about to go up for sale, I discovered a box of our letters in my mother's desk drawer. Some from my grandmother, addressed to me. Some I'd written in return. I marveled at this. Through various moves and purges and life changes, we had saved each other's letters. Somehow, they all ended up in my parents' house, where my mother presciently thought to store them as a single collection.

I didn't know this, though, when I picked up that unlabeled box. I unfolded the cardboard panels and immediately recognized Grandma's handwriting. The first letter I reopened has two blurred and inky water spots where once you could clearly read the words she had written. These dots are not a flaw. They simply compound everything she was trying to say.

I reread every one of those letters, reabsorbing her stories, her curved script swirling through me and marking me with the permanence of pen on paper. Folded into each envelope, along with her letter, was an unwritten message that I'd not understood until that moment:

I took the time to write these pages, crease the paper, lick the envelope, affix the stamp. I formed the script that makes up your name. I remembered your address, by heart. I crunched the gravel down the winding driveway, pulled open the rusty mailbox door, and raised the flag. The postman will come, and he will carry my words to you.

There is a story to share. I've written it for you.

Stages of Grief

Tony Dietz

There was no denying the dog was dead, just as there was no denying the disbelief etched in the little girl's face. Her scream had fled the street. The car, and the screech of its tires, had fled too. Now there was just a man on one side of the road, and a girl on the other, with the silence between them punctuated by a dead dog.

The Phoenix sun bore down on the three. The girl held the handle of a retractable leash in her chubby hands, the leash connecting her to the dog, like the solution to a puzzle in a child's activity book. There was no line connecting the man to either the girl or the dog, and he thought maybe he should keep walking, take off like the driver had. But he didn't. He stood in the hot silence of the street and looked at the dog. A thin trickle of blood made its way across the road to the gutter. He took a pull from the brown-bagged bottle he carried, coughed, then took another pull. Nothing changed. He walked over to the dog and prodded it with the toe of his boot.

"Your dog's dead," he said to the girl.

She glared at him, openly willing him to disappear, willing time to turn back.

The sun burned hot on his neck. The road burned hot through the soles of his boots. He looked at her, then down at the dog, then back at her. She seemed stuck. He cleared his throat and prodded the dog again with his boot.

"Your dog's dead."

"She is not!" Released by hot anger, the girl dropped the leash handle, ran to her dog, and flung her arms about its neck. The handle skittered across the road after her.

The man shifted from foot to foot on the burning pavement. Sweat trickled down his back. His head throbbed. "Can't leave a dead dog in the street," he said. "Gonna have to move it."

"Maybe she can't move cause she's tired." The girl looked up at him, pleading. "Maybe she can't move cause she's sleeping."

"Maybe she can't move cause she's dead."

The girl's eyes started to tear. The man looked away and took a swig from his bottle. "Gonna have to move it," he said. The girl buried her face in her dog's fur and sobbed. The man looked away, squinting out to where the street buckled in a migraine of heat.

The girl's sobs died down. She tugged at her dog's head. "I can't."

"Let me do it." He drained his bottle and placed it on the road beside the dog. He put his battered cardboard sign next to it. The sign read: "Homeless vet—anything helps—even smiles." It was a lie. Smiles never helped.

The dog was lighter than he expected, mostly fluffy coat. Some of its guts stayed on the road. "Where am I taking her?" he asked the girl.

"Daisy was whining for a walk, and Daddy was busy with the people, and Mommy was sleeping, so I took her myself, but there was a bunny and Daisy chased it and a car came and..." She looked down and scuffed her shoe on the road.

"And it hit her, and she died."

The girl nodded and wiped her nose on her sleeve.

"So where am I taking her?"

She pointed down the road to a house whose drive was crowded with cars. More cars lined the street in front.

"Having a party?" he asked the girl.

She didn't answer.

He lugged the dead dog down the street to the house. The girl picked up the leash handle and followed him, the leash now connecting her to the man.

The house was closed and shuttered against the heat, but he could hear a dull murmur of voices above the drone of the air conditioner. He laid the dog in the yard's only shade, under a twisted old mesquite tree. The dog's blood, warm and sticky, had soaked the front of his shirt.

The girl tangled him in the leash as she knelt beside the dog. He tried to unclip it, but his cracked and shaking hands wouldn't cooperate. He had to concentrate, and the effort made his head pound. The leash came loose and struck him in the ear as it whipped back into the handle. He closed his eyes and let out a long breath.

When he stood to go, the girl reached out and grabbed his pant leg.

"What?"

"Will my daddy be mad at me?" Her eyes were solemn and scared.

"Might be."

"I don't want him to be mad, anymore."

"Tell your mom then." He pulled from her grip and started down the path.

"I can't," the girl called after him. "My mommy is sleep—" she searched for the right word. "My mommy is dead."

He stopped.

"That why all these people are here?"

She nodded.

"Ah, shit." His sigh was swallowed by the hot air. He looked about the yard, avoiding the girl's eyes. Geraniums lined the front of the house, bone brittle but for one that persisted in the shade of the mesquite. It offered a single red flower, as improbable as the girl.

She looked up at him, unblinking, her grip white-tight on the handle of a leash that wasn't connected to anything. Her lips trembled, and he thought she might cry again. He looked at the ground. It seemed the cracks in the dirt waited for her tears, yearned for them. His craving sharpened. He would need cardboard for a new sign.

Her voice pulled him back to her. "Maybe you could tell?"

"Tell who?"

"My daddy. He won't be mad if you tell him."

He looked at the girl. Heat snarled in the space between them. He tried to get his mouth around the thing she needed to hear, the thing that would kill the stubborn hope in her eyes.

"Please." Her gaze tugged as hard as her voice.

"Alright," he said.

He climbed the front steps and knocked. As he waited, he felt a hand slide into his, a tiny thing, soft and cool, cradled in his calluses.

Dispatches from Home

Victoria Lynne McCoy

I've been trying to erasure the war reports
into love letters. Pare down the syntax of their weaponry
to a few kind words that taste something akin to you. In your storm-
riddled sleep, the Pacific spits its hollow-bellied melody—
your wounds licked clean of memory, lost scars
wandering the hemispheres of your body. Yesterday's
six-hour flight rerouted around the gale force gusts and I'm just
grateful I got through security without another
man's hands on me. The blizzard sky still ghost-white:
one more item to add to the list of left-behind.
Did you know *desert* comes from *land of the abandoned?*
Country club down the road, bridle trails nestled into hillside,
my childhood home. There are days I tell the wind about you.
This mattress a haunted oasis, your voice a sandstorm
of static. I'm awake, a witness to the slaughter,
night defeated bleeding dust-rose over the bay.

*

The second time you deployed to Iraq
we turned the clocks back. I played the saddest
songs on the stereo. I needed to know my throat
wasn't the only one strung with minor chords. *It's a cold
and it's a broken hallelujah.* I know a girl who stole the key
to the gun locker of her first lover, wears it around her neck,
but you have always been my favorite trigger. I've stared down
the hollows of too many 6 a.m.'s, light slipping
through the paper-cut horizon. If you let a fire burn long enough,
will it consume its loneliness? Praise the day preoccupied with ending
because it hasn't ended yet. I wash my hair in hallelujah.
I will kiss you hallelujah when you return. You,
accidental city, you Pyrrhic victory of a city. My body knows
when it is a stopover, but not how to turn the hungry away.

*

Hasn't there always been a need for the wounded?
Silhouettes at the cliff's edge shatter in the swagger
of dawn-water. In us, a desert we can't dance off.
Don't abandon me, sweet mirage. Can't you see: you are
both the fist and the clenching. My heart is a paper cup city
in the beggar hands of the world, never full, but what small change
it contains constantly clanks out some semblance of music.
My heart is a treasonous plot to take over my rational thought
but everyone's busy watching the parade. A wilderness contained
outside my window. The day gaining on itself,
the gold-strewn trees buckling. I miss the house
your breath builds around me. I can't tell anymore
which part of me is the wound, and which part the need.

In the Skies Above Southwest Oklahoma
Ryan Clark

For Altus Air Force Base, Oklahoma

1. *In the Skies Above Southwest Oklahoma*
Activate us
as an engine of flight
in a war-held area
heaving men young into the air
and then nothing.

A military is soon a land
prepared for ache
and wide of fences.

We gather a guard
station as the ideal
location for a mouth,
a heavy rifle tongue,
and we trace
with a jet-
fueled finger
our dawn.

2. *Altus Army Airfield*
All this air pulses
deep with history.

We light the fuel of it,
shooting into World War II
a flight school, and a love
of firmament.

For an airfield drags
us back with landing,
is a deal with
the air to return.

A base is among friends:
we are safe if
we are touching.

A pilot is a honed
skill raining aircraft
with hands of care,
this AT-9 and
this AT-7 singing
capable through
furious winds.

This assigned operation
hovers ready over the prairie,
over the red earth, over
fields of cotton and us.

3. *Your Yes Vote on the Air School Will Help Whip Hitler*
Run this sentence
as a banner headlong
on the page.

Altus is a membrane
of a struck body,
zeroes vocalized forceful
of memory, and the sign
is a ledger of Altus'
backing the vote.

There is proof in a count of
five hundred seventy five to ten,
in our X on the ballot,
as if victory is a choice of
land here.

4. *From Growing Cotton to Graduating Pilots in Eleven Months!*
The work of form,
of clawed dirt set
in a level surface,
of the heaving rust-
stung equipment
hot in a field—here
we are laid out
in rows of barracks
and office buildings
sprung up as a
water tower and
telephone lines.

We are strong in such concrete.
We are a fort with sides.

The field was red, is
shaved in a way of repair,
and we are erected
on the edges.

A runway is a line
we extend from the city
to the sky; a warehouse
for catching what returns
is made a hangar.

Our occupancy is everyone
alive in this built day.

5. *Satellite Airstrips*
The air is an untrusted
auxiliary field, nervously
holding us skirted
off the floor, stripes
arranged in rivers of vapor.

Into isolated fields
we rush scenes
of vicious human error,
caustic rash of charred
plains, unauthorized stunts
faced with the truth
of falling, of the fragility
in an all-metal,
twin engine lung.

6. *A Graveyard for Surplus Aircraft*
At the end of a hostile Europe,
Altus Army Airfield is a place
on a map inactive, meaning
unfought surface, or a fist
opened to feel
whatever's left over.

Merrily with bombers
and fighters civilians

strip the plane soluble
into what we
return as hope
in manageable pieces.

Salvage a local recall—
of radios soft
among workers prying
open steel-
dressed wings,
of the process of bolt-
stripping, gripping
copper wires
full in the hand,
of our reach of crane
with the five-foot
metal blade that moved
like the slow shrug
of another body.

On the planet, then,
the bulldozer pushes
forward, where
melting aluminum
bares no picture.

7. *Training Begins Again*
Eight years after salvage
rifled through traces
of sky clung to wings,
the jet engine
powered the base as a
face stretched back
to waking.

See our regular use
of in-flight refueling,
this zeroing in
of artificial limbs
in the air. Trust
the song of reach
even above so much
empty space.

Here, full
of reservoir, we
reactivate.

8. *A New Mission: Air Transport*
We are a force
expanding, held
onto wars
sure of a mission, air
transporting in and
shoved out.

The running of our fist
as a cargo aircraft huge
in star fields
is only a faint flash
of red dots
fording the cover of night.

Into this I arrive a body
in the skies above
Southwest Oklahoma.

I won't forget

now that I reach
back for it; are

our cargo openings
fastened tight,
to be ferried over
a further becoming?

9. *Port of Debarkation*
From August 1990 through
March 1991 we are a
fortified area
of fathers
leaving as soldiers
into a desert.

Packages arrive
as return;
we find a shirt
and a few
read-for-sure letters.

One day we see
a few silver MREs
and we eat.

10. *Altus AFB 2012 Economic Impact*
Under Altus AFB is a steady
heart, a refueling of
economic capacity
through the gated aorta
and full into the rush of body
collecting, this land
we are tied to.
Made here and leaving
we are a fast change
of veins and arteries
active and inactive.

HOMECOMING

ASHLEY HAND

Emmett put his bags down on the floor and dropped to his knees. The bulldog was peeing, on Emmett's hands, on the pant leg of his uniform. Her nails scrabbled across the hardwood as she spun in circles and jumped to lick his face.

You're a good girl, he said to the dog.

She's happy to see you, Adrienne said.

I'm going to shower, he said.

Okay.

I'll get the rest of my stuff out of the car when I'm done.

I can get it.

Leave it for me.

Okay.

Adrienne stood in the entryway. Dust floated in the late afternoon sunshine filtering in through the windows. At 6 a.m., she'd hauled the Shop-Vac out of the basement and sucked up the little balls of hair and lint and skin that had accumulated along the baseboards, the dirt in the dining room from the plants she'd recently potted. She'd made a cup of coffee in the Keurig and walked around the house for twenty minutes holding the hose out in front of her, suctioning the dust out of the air and into the little tank. Emmett would want to come home to a clean house. She made another cup of coffee, and another. She shouldn't have had any. She was nervous. She needed a Xanax. But she couldn't drive if she took a Xanax.

Adrienne heard the rush of water come alive in the walls. Her eyelids felt heavy. She'd glued fake eyelashes to her real eyelashes that morning, after cleaning. It cost $100 to get them done profession-ally, so she bought a strip for $5.99 from Walgreens. She'd propped a mirror against a houseplant on the kitchen counter and sidled up to it with a pair of tweezers and fancy superglue that was safe to put next to her eyeballs. The trick was to do the eyelashes one at a time. She'd watched a YouTube video that said you couldn't plunk a cluster of three or five onto one eyelash because your real eyelash would get heavy and fall out. You had to take one false eyelash with a pair of tweezers and dunk it in the glue and then line it up properly so the swoop was going in the right direction and then place it carefully on your real eyelash and then wait for ten seconds for it to dry and then do the next one, so on and so forth, about eighty times each eye. *Grey's Anatomy* was playing in the background. She made it through three episodes.

After the eyelashes, she curled her hair. Put on lipstick. It was the kind that you could still wear if you planned to kiss someone. She'd kissed the meat of her hand between her thumb and index finger to test it out.

She'd waited in the hangar for over an hour for his plane to land. Emmett had hugged her and kissed her cheek when he stepped out onto the concrete tarmac. She told him he could kiss her on the lips but he said, Your lipstick, and she said, It won't come off, and he said, Are you ready to head home? and now here she was still waiting in the hallway for him to get out of the shower and for them to make love and for it to feel normal again.

An email, a few weeks into his deployment:

I feel separated from the entire world. No other person I know has been here. They've barely heard of it. The hadji cook thaws the meat out in his car on the drive back from the city. I could disappear and nobody would be able to place their finger where I was on the map.

The emails got shorter and more spaced apart. Emmett was on missions at night, outside the wire, camping on the scrubby Afghan desertscape with eighty pounds of gear.

Adrienne mailed boxes with freeze-dried stroganoff and spaghetti Emmett could heat up over his JetBoil. She attached love notes on

Post-Its to the packaging. She trolled Al Jazeera for news. November 7, three US troops were killed and three others wounded in an IED blast near Ghazni. She knew Emmett's tiny base was somewhere in that region. She sent him an email with a photo of the bulldog wearing a too-tight sweater.

Hope all is well, love you.

Adrienne woke up in the night with fears of bombs, explosions. She drove five minutes to the gas station for menthols and sat on the curb smoking to calm down. She heard from him on November 9.

Did you remember to call someone and have the sprinklers blown out?

She owned a house on the other side of Albuquerque. She'd bought it before she and Emmett were married, before she'd moved into his home with its blue Mexican tiles and terra cotta floors and alabaster stucco walls at the base of the Sandías. Her house was crumbly and old. She bought it because of the chimney, and the wood siding, and the covered porch. It had character, and also she couldn't afford anything better. She spent the entire summer renovating it. She peeled up seven layers of vinyl flooring to expose the original wood underneath. She rented an industrial sander to grind off the glue and paint splatters, then waxed and polished them herself. She knocked down walls. She built walls. She trimmed windows. She removed toilets and tiled bathroom floors. She made herself broke on that house. She loved that house. It was in a bad area. She could hear sirens at night when she was trying to fall asleep. She installed locks on all of the windows and a home security system. She built a fence around the small property so that she didn't have to look at the neighbors, the paunchy wives and barefoot children. She could have lived in that house forever and never come out. Now it was rented out to a family with small children who probably pooped in the bathtub and smeared jam on the walls. She wished it was empty.

Adrienne sat on the sofa and waited. The water shut off in the bathroom. She heard Emmett moving about on the tile floor. Then it went quiet. She stood. She would go join him, kiss his body, touch the whole, intact pieces of him, take him in her mouth. She felt tears sliding out of the corners of her eyes. She sat back down. She would stay put. She tucked herself under a blanket. She looked around for the bulldog. Had the dog gone in the bedroom with Emmett?

She put her head down on an upholstered oblong pillow. She focused on her meditations, her breathing. She fell asleep. When she awoke, there was a note on the counter.

Went for a run.

You don't go back to normal life so easily, you just don't, Adrienne told her sister later on the phone, when Emmett had been away for upwards of an hour on his run and Adrienne found herself at loose ends, not wanting to leave the house in case he returned. She kept the oven preheated. Steaks were marinating in the fridge. It was okay, Adrienne said, she would stand by Emmett until they survived and got to whatever was on the other side, and her sister said, oh sweetheart, and Adrienne said, it's okay, and her sister said, do you think it would be easier if it wasn't just you two, if there were kids, and   Adrienne felt the tears again. She said she had to go and could she call her sister back later, and then she sat at the kitchen table and waited for the sound of the front door.

After Reading Reports from the California Wildfires, Six Weeks Before My Father's Overdose

Erik Wilbur

Somewhere, my father drinks from veins
of fallen leaves, he termites
the downed logs of his life. The fire that will take
him starts as smoke rising
from pine-litter. He knows he can't survive,
so he's been leaving empty vodka bottles on the floor of his truck,
answering the phone high, signaling us
to say what we need to say
and leave him. We see the smoke,
but we don't leave, and we can't say everything. Instead,
I filter inhales through my shirt and imagine
switch-backing ashy hillsides
to practice forgiveness. I wonder how
the displaced in California will forgive
the aerated limbs of dead oaks and the late-summer
wind that carried embers up to their roofs.
No matter how many lies addicts tell us, an overdose is
an act of honesty. In time, it seems as natural as a sapling.
And who couldn't forgive a sapling, even as it grows in ash,
even if it becomes embers in the wind.

Because of Course: An Award-Winning Story

Mike Karpa

I am going to win a prize. I will write a story that has a prosperous, middle-aged male protagonist who is white and from somewhere between Maine and Minnesota, maybe somewhere as far south as Maryland, but definitely one of the M states, or their immediately adjacent neighbors. But not Montana, not Missouri, and certainly not Mississippi. Unless he is some sort of no-hoper, a drinker, under-educated, three-and-a-half natural teeth, no ambition, etc., though still middle aged and white. But no, my guy will be from the right set of M states. He'll be married, a second marriage, to a somewhat younger spouse, female. *She* will be from the wrong set of M states, but will have escaped before she lost her teeth.

The sex they have will be the kind that doesn't lose you your job or get you beat up. It will be mentioned, but have no details, because the details of it will not threaten their lives or livelihoods. They will have always lived with the expectation that they will be able to have sex as they please. He will have a reverie about a young woman ("the Girl"[1]) who spent languid hours with him talking about MacArthur dreams at the Oxbridge bedsit he lived in when finishing a Fulbright after his summer at the Yaddo Colony, all of which he abandons to become an NYU film professor. He will have connections, a quirky

---

[1] Niobh, who he thinks works in a café and whom he calls "Nayobi," thinking this is funny. She finds this faux-hickness endearing at first, a disguise for his insecurities. He doesn't know Niobh has been accepted to Oxbridge and starts in the fall and she doesn't tell him, expecting he would find it threatening, which he would. She will come to find "Nayobi"

European car, a man-bun, and some crucial possession he and his second wife—younger than his first by a tasteful amount, six years—shouldn't have bought because it's really expensive and they can't afford it.

And children. They will have children. Two, one from each of his marriages. The older child will hate his or her parents or be distancing himself/herself from them. Maybe because the parents keep rabbiting on about how they can't afford the possession. Only they keep not selling off the possession, so really they *can* afford it, which is a relief to the reader, because the reader has expensive possessions that the reader fears losing. And all four—mother, father, child, other child—will have names that the reader has heard of and work in places she's heard of and do things she's heard of, only these will be names, places, and things that the reader has not herself encountered except in Pushcart stories.

The mother and father will have affairs that they regret. They will treasure their regret. They will compare their regret to the regrets of others. They will each separately make new friends with whom they gleefully and at last bare their mistakes in bars as they drink moderately. Their new friends will be from the wrong set of M states, respectively, but conveniently only be passing through, leaving no obligations that derail the story. The father will drive very fast in a too-powerful car, not his own, probably at the end of the story, and that will show something to the reader about freedom, or the lack of it. There will be no resonant simulacra, no red herrings or mysteries. Except for why life is so meaningless. No, not meaningless, just a sense that it's not worth all that much or valuable to them because it has all come easy. But not too easy, because they have had feelings along the way. Not regret, though. That comes later, after the affairs. Or between affairs. And they won't be addicted to anything. Not even cell phones.

The distancing child, a daughter, will resent her younger half-sibling, a toddler, who the mother/stepmother will take to an expensive preschool or private kindergarten where other mothers will gossip

---

unamusing by the end, shouting "Neeve, Neeve," as they break up in the café where she doesn't work.

He will edit this from his memories of the summer.

that the mother/stepmother is not doing something right. Secretly, each of the other mothers will fear she may be replaced by a younger woman, as their friend the previous wife was. The daughter will be oddly friendly with her stepmother. The daughter will not know about her stepmother's affair, but the daughter *will* know about the father's affair, which is with a girl, like "the Girl" one day past the age of consent, like he is French or Woody Allen. Or no, make it three or four years, because ick. In fact, maybe his lover is a woman who is not only older than his current wife, but older than his previous wife, and only a few years shy of being older than his mother, perhaps a free-spirited friend of his mother, named, say, Maude, and yes, we are thinking here of Harold &, and a priest flecking spittle and talking of "withered flesh." Because twist! And the daughter looks up to her grandmother's friend/father's lover Maude, because twist! Daughter, stepmother, father and toddler will live in a beautiful apartment in New York, probably Brooklyn, no, not an apartment, a whole brownstone, probably in Park Slope, that is in fine shape, despite nobody ever working on it, except for one thing that's always breaking and getting repaired, but not very well.

The stepmother will be on the verge of middle-age, despite her toddler, and ache with the desire to point out to the older, gossipy, other-mother chorus that *she* is not middle-aged. Although really she is. Readers will enjoy this, because they will know she is middle-aged and yet take her as proof that they are not themselves middle-aged. She will have lost another child in her youth, in an earlier marriage, neither fact has she shared with her genuinely middle-aged husband, because secrets!

Either he or she will have a parent, probably a mother—of course a mother, *his* mother—who is a famous *artiste*, narcissistic and controlling, stroppy, upon whom they are dependent, though not for child care. The idea! The *artiste* grandmother may, perhaps, own the brownstone. The resentful, distancing daughter will feel a strong connection to her *artiste* grandmother, unaware this sentiment is not returned.

They may all travel to Europe together, for the controlling grandmother's retrospective. The grandmother is much less famous than she was, but someone in Barcelona remembers her fondly and has assembled a show in a sunlit gallery on La Rambla, tracking down all the collectors who bought the grandmother's major pieces, which is difficult because those collectors are not currently as wealthy as they should've been/were expected to become, and some even live in the wrong set of M states. It would have been interesting if those less-than-wealthy collectors had banded together with the grandmother to clandestinely fund this show in an unethical attempt to boost the value of their collections, but that is too close to crime, and there is no crime in the story. If it were a novel, there might be a bank robbery or a tasteful but bloody murder, really bloody, but it is not a novel; it is a Pushcart story.

When the clan assembles in Barcelona, tempers will flare due to a high-status exigency—that longed-for MacArthur glory, an inheritance, marriage to a Vanderbilt, something like that arousing intense envy, maybe even jealousy. The tensions will ascend toward the opening at Galeria La Rambla, now broadcasting electric light into the Catalan night. Overflow crowds will talk in a loud rumble of incoherent snatches—*people* are *nicer there … who* wouldn't *want to … I don't think we can make a* rhubarb *Negroni*—until someone wanders off, probably the toddler, whose portrait is the featured "new work" of the retrospective, the only red-dot opportunity.

The mother will go insane with worry, because this is also how she lost her previous child. Here it will be revealed that the previous child disappeared and was never found, hinting that the child is still alive, and the reader will hope for a melodramatic reappearance of the now-adult child and all secrets being revealed. The controlling grandmother will, apparently at random, paraphrase Oscar Wilde—to lose one parent may be regarded as a misfortune; to lose both looks like carelessness—hinting at knowledge of the missing previous child, achieved, one might surmise, in the course of her controlling.

Of course, no secrets will be revealed. The grandmother will be cruel, the father will start a new doomed affair, the mother will want to leave him but defer, since she is consumed with the hunt for her newly missing child. As the adults confront each other with their rather ordinary failings, the daughter will, canvassing La Rambla on her own, encounter the toddler and decide to flee with her young sister. How the daughter will fund this will not be explained, but wealthy relatives may be hinted at.

France will be involved, of course, because *artiste*. They will all speak French. Entire sentences in French will be sprinkled through the story, never translated or explained. Maybe the daughter and toddler will meet a nameless Arab in a train station (called "the Arab,"[2] even though he's French) as the two head north through the Pyrenees, there being a need for a brown supporting character. He will not be evil, because that is not tasteful, but he may be flavorless, and his personal history will be mentioned only as it pertains to the New York family—perhaps he was a child extra in a movie the father taught in his classes, *Babel* or *The Sheltering Sky*.[3]

The father's affairs will not be discovered, but merely sensed, but that will be enough for the mother to leave him, not because she is angry, but because she feels no inclination to stay. She will be haunted by her second lost child, but feel rather than tragedy a general sense of Wildean carelessness amidst a conviction that all three children will return to her, including her stepdaughter, because she may never forgive her stepdaughter—will never forgive her step-daughter—but at heart she trusts her to take good care of her sister, and also because come on! How much can she be expected to take? She will miss the gossip of the other mothers. It turns out that pariah might not be the greatest status, but it beats no status. Now she will feel middle-aged.

The father, now also down a couple children, will be fired by the university and forced to take a demeaning but high-paying job, perhaps in finance. This is when he will take that high-speed car ride and obliquely reveal that he and his first wife, who adored the man-bun, did not divorce, as the reader was tricked into assuming, but rather she died, of cancer of course—a miserable few years—and that he and Maude never had sex, although they did get naked once, and the reader can give a sigh of relief, because withered flesh. And

---

[2] Ihsan, a recent university graduate in electrical engineering who introduces himself to the daughter as "Ethan" because she speaks only English. He is on his way home after a job search in Madrid, where he had expected to get more of a fair hearing in job interviews than he has in Paris, which he did, but was nonetheless undone by a lack of facility in Spanish.
[3] None of Ihsan's Madrid interviewers, unfortunately, saw either movie.

the new doomed affair will give way to a relationship with a hotshot analyst named Jane Peter Herbert who makes more money than he does and replaces him with a younger man because nothing that will ever happen to him will be surprising, because man-bun. Although perhaps he and Maude really loved each other and were attracted to each other, because he's getting a bit withered himself at this point, to be honest, and because twist!

The grandmother will turn out to have in fact had a colluding-collector scheme (which may mean the story only gets a Pushcart nomination, not an actual prize, depending on the number of adverbs, even if used adroitly) and the scheme will succeed despite its unmasking, or perhaps because of it, earning the grandmother notoriety that translates into more power over her son and daughter-in-law. Everyone will hate her for this, even the unrequitedly bonded granddaughter in Paris. All three—that is, stepmother, father and grandmother—will get smaller but still lovely apartments in different parts of New York, like Hell's Kitchen or Williamsburg or Chelsea, places the reader has heard of but couldn't find on a map if a gun were held to her head. One of the three may be exiled to Jamaica Plain, or maybe Rehoboth, but Rehoboth only if it's the stepmother, who decides[4] she's lesbian. She listens to Les Rita Mitsouko as she walks the beach wondering when her daughters will return—*La sagesse aménage... Les rides font leurs traces*—although if she's serious about sex with women she won't get to be in any more Pushcart stories.

The same broken thing will be broken in all three of the new apartments, but not in the twenty-first arrondissement apartment of the daughter and her toddler sister that Maude is renting for them from "the Arab's" likewise nameless parents[5].

---

[4] *Decides*, because although she's been attracted to women since adolescence, she hopes pretending to have discovered this only now, as though stumbling on a beguiling shell at the beach, will calm the sensibilities of the straight other mothers, whom she rightly expects to bristle at the notion that the threat of violence and ostracism *from them* might have kept her in the closet.

[5] Amal and Nabil, both communist, both bakers, refugees who fled Benghazi before their son and subsequent twin girls were born. They are bakers still, and live below the apartment they rent to Maude. Their ownership of the four-story building does not interfere with their anti-capitalist beliefs, but rather feels like a baguette-fueled triumph over capitalism that they find amusing and laugh about over long cozy dinners with family and friends, dinners which come to include the daughter and her toddler sister, who later are invited less frequently as Ihsan gets exhausted and frustrated being the only one who understands everything that is going on and yet unable himself to speak because he is constantly interpreting for people with arguably less to say.

The reader will now intuit the other mothers are afraid not of being replaced by a second wife, but of dying like the first wife. Because life hasn't come so easy after all, has it? The missing previous child will never appear, and the reader will tell herself that she is glad, because she didn't really hope for that because she likes literary fiction not melodrama.

That will be a lie.

What the reader never learns, is that the missing previous child is alive and well and living in Memphis, selling souvenirs on Mud Island, which is where she met her boyfriend, a strong and ethical fellow with good hair. The two live within their means, fostering senior dogs, and generally having a lot of harmless fun. And in idle moments, when there are no Mud Island customers clamoring for machine-embroidered visors and fried dough and she has time to watch the Mississippi flow muddily down from Tennessee to Arkansas, neither an M state, she does find that, despite her easy happiness, she misses the mom that she can no longer remember.

And in Rehoboth, finally, a postcard arrives, to be clutched and re-read kneeling on the beach as the tide rolls in: Come to Paris. Because if we are writing the story, if we have a choice, why not opt for happy? And adverbs.

HERETIC

CATE McGOWAN

Last night, on the 7:00 p.m. news, some helmet-haired anchor whimpered as she warned viewers: "And in local news, a rare spitting cobra is on the loose." The blonde reporter bared her tombstone teeth as she hissed her distaste and leaned into the camera, whispering, "I just don't like snakes!"

This morning, Connie worries. Special bulletins still scroll across the bottom of her TV screen: *A deadly cobra's escaped. Be on the lookout when you're outdoors! If you make visual contact, keep your distance and call Florida Fish and Wildlife.*

She wonders about the snake. It's hiding somewhere, stealthing through shadows, slithering under palmetto and scrub weeds. She imagines it slinking past speed walkers, striking at yappy dogs tied up in backyard pens.

But Connie's got bigger problems. She needs a hard fix—she's waited too long. She searches through her mother's junk drawers, digs between sofa cushions, but her fingers emerge empty and sticky, coated in crumbs. Her hunt yields shit. Nothing. No pills, no powder.

In the hallway, the cuckoo clucks twelve noon, but it feels like thirteen o'clock. She pukes into the sink, then calls her connection.

"Um, on my way," he mumbles. She knows he isn't coming soon.

Her mother's cat, Elbert, pops in through the open side window. He twines between her legs, whirligigs on his back, and she leans down, rakes her fingers down his spine.

She lights a drag and inhales deeply, tucks a can of lighter fluid into her back pocket.

"It's dangerous out there, buddy…there's a snake." She finds a beach towel wadded on the couch, fashions a sling over her shoulder, hoists Elbert into the improvised hammock.

"Come on, boy. You're safer with me."

Her mother, in bed as always, hollers after her.

"Constance, you going out?" Connie slams the door without answering, hesitates on the bright stoop, sidesteps across the yard through weeds. There's a zipping in her head like a song on repeat, and she stiffens her spine as she strolls down the middle of the unshaded street. Elbert squirms in his makeshift swath. His head peeks out and bobs with each step.

No one's safe. Everyone's afraid of poison, of the unknown. Folks in the neighborhood have closed up their shutters. There's not a small child in sight. She watches jittery lunch-break dog walkers flock together on the corner under the shade of a giant bird of paradise. An old couple jogs past her with their beagles on short leads. A kid furiously pedals his bike, swerves with speed down the lake slope. And some lady in sparkling high tops, lips smeared with pink gloss, scuffles close to Connie, tugs a poodle on a chain. High Top Lady looks right, then left, nervous. Connie tries a smile, and High Top Lady squeaks at her.

"You OK out here in your *condition?*"

High Top Lady side-eyes Connie's swollen midsection, bruised and scabby forearms, the half-burned-down butt, bundled cat. Connie flushes, tugs her T-shirt over her protruding navel, flicks her cigarette into the grass. The lady winces and clucks in distaste, yanks her wiry dog, U-turns, crosses the street. Connie flips her a bird.

"Hey, fuck you, old lady!"

Elbert purrs as Connie walks faster now, nestles on the ledge of her bulbous belly. She turns the corner, makes it to the cul-de-sac.

At the dead end, an oak tree, centuries old, holds court in the park. Some developer has spray-painted a yellow X on its thick trunk. The area, even the tree, is slated for clearing. All the grove's border palms and underbrush are already shorn to nubs. Nothing is left but the tree and some weeds.

She sifts and side-winds through the sugar sand, and when she pushes under the looming oak's branches, she parts the limbs like she'd lift a veil. Under the boughs' cool awning, where it's quiet as a church nave, she nuzzles Elbert's forehead, sits on a low branch, imagines that a loose serpent curves inside fern beds farther out in the woods beyond the fence. She conjures a scene of the liberated cobra rising up on its coiled, anchored body, its hood a spoon. The snake strikes at some squirrel running past.

Elbert sighs in his sling, snuggles into her neck, and she pats his bundled body, thinks about how knowledge and knowing are different things.

Only five months ago, she'd shared this spot with Christopher, and together, they'd straddled this low V crook. In a lull punctuated only by carking jays and crikes, she'd carved his name with a key, cursiving the letters into the bark with care, fashioning the beginnings of a heart, whittling a swoop around his name.

As she scraped the trunk's surface, she spoke. "What's inside me. It's …"

But he quieted her, placed his thick hand on her thigh. "You're just … weird …" His voice trailed off—she could hear something like irritation or disgust in his tone. She wasn't sure what it was. Christopher gazed up at the sky then, looking through the leaves; shade moved over his face; light peeked through the foliage and tattooed green patterns over his cheeks. She'd never seen anything so beautiful.

And then he spoke again. He curled his lip, repeating his first pronouncement. This time the declaration was decisive: "Yep, you're really weird, and you got no purpose."

He stood up, smoothed his big hands down his stained khakis, adjusted his belt, and shambled away. He didn't glance back.

She watched his Toyota thump toward the forked curve, take a left, and he was gone for good. And she'd never had the opportunity to tell him what was inside her.

Now, from her tree perch, Connie tries to push away all that stuff. She looks out at the road, the heat deciding everything. Some snake's weaving a question out there with venom in the clock-ticking grass. Anyway, she knows danger's camouflaged in plain sight. Satellite dishes and smartphones, the straitjacket of paychecks and spreadsheets, the prick of needles and fake bliss at the end of a point.

She remembers Sunday school lessons.

"Class, *somebody*, explain the two trees in Eden."

The snake. The Devil's disguise. The couple. Eve didn't select wisely. Connie would not have picked the Tree of Knowledge's apple. Some things are more important than a tree or its fruit.

Now, she traces the relief of that half-finished heart from five months ago. She stands, reaches into her jeans pocket for the lighter fluid she's brought, then flips the top and squeezes the can, squirts a stream into the canopy above, sparks her Bic, then tosses it and the can into the oak, flings them high. The tree bursts orange. It explodes. *Zoooosh!*

Acorns pop loud as gunshots, and Elbert awakens, antennas his ears, then flattens them and growls; his vibrations push through Connie.

"It's OK, boy. Heat rises."

She crouches and rubs her aching abdomen. Her head's bloated with a loud trumpet buzz, but for a moment longer, she watches the conflagration grow. The fire spreads the same way affection overtakes a person.

In the tree, crackles give way to roars. She pats Elbert, who is shifting and whining, backs away from the pyrotechnics, turns, strides home. The rhythm of her pace calms him, and he slackens.

Halfway down the block, she pivots. The oak's fully aflame now. A spectacle. Its blazing limbs arrow to the ground. Flares stab the sky, and the dark ash spirals over the entire neighborhood. A shroud of smoldering dust settles on housetops, on the tree-line.

A snake's gone missing, and a fire takes a tree. The world smells black.

Connie scrubs the W stripe between Elbert's sleeping eyes. The skin on her torso twitches, and sweat trickles down her thighs. Something clicks off inside her.

Emergency vehicles speed past now, their sirens bellowing a sad tune. Sure, her connection's coming in a little while, and it'll douse that orchestra buzz in her head, but for the rest of her baby's life, she'll worry about that serpent. It's thirteen o'clock. She wishes she could turn the time back to twelve.

Dear Anhedonia

Carrie McGath
AWP Intro Journals Award winner

Dear Anhedonia,

For all he knows, I wasn't trying to save a life,
a tiny curled up black shadow just starting to breathe.

Maybe these terrible men of ours
were meant to be, so we would be

meant to be. But what are the chances?
Something as old-fashioned as talk radio,

us calling in like injured larks,
whispering to the woman with a drawl

and unremarkable advice connecting us.
We were both in our own locked spaces.

Me in the backseat of the car in a closed garage,
you in the walk-in cooler at work, framed by cattle ribs

hanging like silenced harps.
You bribed your boss with head to let you in there

to call the program, *Dinah at Midnight,*
then to call me, outlining the plan.

As I write this tonight, I imagine the distance to you.
I would kiss your cheeks, each of them

equally, unequivocally, and hug your aching body
against my Midwestern-cool Ohio skin.

Imagining this, I would smell the blood
of the slaughter on your skin and you would smell him

and his motor oiled coveralls on me. I called in:
If your husband won't even take his filthy coveralls off ...

Dinah at Midnight said, *The romance is gone,*
hey doll? Her drawl vibrated the radio signals

and moved right through me as I thought,
I must die. Maybe just kill him. Rape. Hate.

Hurt. I interrupt Dinah, *The yearning*
is true. I riddle with bullets.

Anhedonia, I see you in my rouged cheeks:
a pink like primrose vulvas, aiming to be happy.

My pink-red-salmon face is from sleepless nights,
filled with thoughts of you. And your last letter:

Meet me in the desert. I leave tomorrow.
I will get everything ready for you.

I tell you Yes, yes.
We are both brunettes and must

stick together with a bravery in our bras.
Do not let anyone tell you otherwise, ever.

I already feel so close to you, almost feeling
the sand, the heat, the saddles. I leave in 3 days.

But maybe you shouldn't listen to a word I say
today. My face looks like an eggplant

and I am bleeding, so I sit on old newspapers,
staining them like a puppy. I am careful

not to use the Personals section or his Sports section.
He says I never think about him. His needs.

But I like the Personals
and he said I will get the soap

in the sock again if I fucked with his Sports section.
But last night, I used it to line a little box in the garage,

making a nest for an injured black squirrel.
For all he knows, I threw his Sports away accidentally.

For all he knows, I wasn't trying to save a life,
a tiny curled up black shadow just starting to breathe.

Those little claws framing Monday's football scores,
that little tail pointing to the results of the NFL draft.

I hope you can move in 3 days, little shadow.
Soon, we will be safe in her arms,

hidden in the sand
finally safe from almost every man.

VISITATION

JEN SAMMONS
AWP INTRO JOURNALS AWARD WINNER

The desk attendant taps long purple fingernails on the counter while I sign my name on a clipboard labeled "Visitors." *You know, the first time you came, I thought you were a social worker,* she says.

What's the last name, again? She locates my file, then shakes gold bangles down one arm, and leans back on her elbow, considering me. *You're always dressed so nice and you just don't seem like ... you know ...*

I want to scream. *Like someone who doesn't have custody of her child?* Yeah, I KNOW. I'm not supposed to be here. All four of us are supposed to be at home, the children laughing and playing, secure in the finality of their adoption, far away from social workers and case plans. I'm supposed to be finishing up dinner—something hearty for fall—a beef roast pulled sizzling from the oven, now resting on the counter, maybe. Potatoes and carrots soaking up the juices, becoming so filled that they split apart, overcome with richness, warmth.

Instead, my wife and our son are at home microwaving leftover pasta, and I'm here clutching foil-wrapped tacos in a paper bag waiting to have a court-ordered visitation with our daughter.

It's our fall festival tonight! The desk attendant gestures toward a cardboard box of pumpkins. She explains how my daughter (do I still get to call her that?) and I can each pick out a pumpkin before we leave. *We have something special each month,* she says. *In November we'll have a turkey craft.*

In July Jo and I checked our daughter into a children's mental health in-patient program "due to homicidal actions toward caregivers and abusive actions toward three-year-old brother."

In August we went to court to voluntarily give Children's Services temporary custody of our daughter in an act of desperation and hope for all four members of our family.

In September I met her new foster parents.

Today, pumpkins. November, turkeys.

December will be our final visit.

I retreat to the predictability of the molded plastic waiting area chairs. Check my watch. Wonder if she's safe. Wonder if she's excited. Wonder if she might like the pale green silk scarf I'm wearing. The one that probably reminded the attendant that I don't look like I belong on this side of the desk. I unlock my phone. No messages. It's getting dark. Where are they? Breathe. They're probably stuck in traffic. Breathe. It'll be okay. Use a coping tool. Text a friend. Ames. Breathe.

                         Hey

I type, pressing 4 twice for "h," 3 twice for "e" and hitting 9 three times for "y." I don't need an upgrade. There's nothing wrong with this phone.

What're you up to?
                         Hi there! Waiting for
                         a session to start at the
                         FemRhet conference. You?
Waiting for visitation
at Children's Services.
Wanna trade?
                         LOL! No.
                         That must be hell. I'm sorry.

The door opens. I shove my phone in my pocket and look up. She's here! My daughter. In this moment, every fear, every violent episode, every scream, every terror, fades away—renders itself into the chill of the October air as the door closes behind them.

Hi sweetheart! I'm so glad to see you! She grins. She's lost another tooth. She's taller too. I hold out the size 7 purple ski jacket we picked out together at a mom-to-mom sale two springs ago. I had promised that even though it was too big then, she would definitely grow into it someday. *It's cold outside! I thought you might like to have this.*

She grins again, clutches it to her chest. *My jacket! Thanks, Mama!*

My breath catches. She still gets to call me that.

The foster dad clears his throat. *Do you know if there's a Burger King around here?* This is an improvement. Last month he wouldn't speak to me at all. I give him directions to Wendy's and Taco Bell, feeling inadequate. He sighs. *That'll have to do, I guess.*

He doesn't say goodbye. I've yet to see him smile. Twenty-four hours from now I'll be on the phone with the caseworker letting her know that my daughter spent the first half of our visitation in the bathroom, sick.

Did you eat anything on the way here? I ask her, from outside the bathroom stall.

Doritos, she cries. *Mr. --- bought them for me. My belly hurts so bad, Mama!*

She's allergic to dairy.

When I relay this to the caseworker the next day, she sighs. *Well, what did you expect?*

When my daughter is able to leave the bathroom, I buy her a Sprite from the vending machine to settle her stomach, and we walk hand in hand to the room we have been assigned this time. They're all the same: small table and chairs, easy-to-clean couch, books with ripped pages, that toy with wooden beads that slide along metal roller-coaster tracks. We eat the (dairy-free) tacos, play UNO, chat about school. Our interactions today are easy, light. So different from the horrors we lived at home together.

June: Broken furniture, scissors as weapons, our three-year-old's disclosure of what his sister had been doing to him.

October: It's been four months since she lived with us, but still he barely sleeps. Mostly screams. Is ripping out his own eyebrows.

February: Jo and I will be in court again, voluntarily surrendering parental rights of our daughter in order to protect both children.

They are incredibly traumatized, I'll tell the judge. *She was horrifically abused in the foster home before she came home to us. What she's doing to her brother is what she knows. It is equally terrifying for both children each time she acts. They cannot live safely in the same home.*

We've played five rounds of UNO and read all the books. I suggest Go Fish and she starts to whine. The second hour of visitation always begins to feel like waiting for a doctor's appointment that never happens. I dig in my purse for a box of restaurant crayons and we decorate an unused napkin from the taco bag. Finally, the desk attendant appears in the doorway and taps her watch. *Time to go pick your pumpkins!*

Do you want to pick a pumpkin? I ask my daughter. She shrugs.

The desk attendant turns to her. *Come on, baby. Mr. --- will be back any minute now!*

I don't want to let him take her. I want to take my daughter by the hand and start running toward our car. What if we've made a mistake? What if there's another way to make this work?

June: We met with Children's Services to make a plan. *You could have her live in residential care and just come home for holidays*, they said. *That way she'd be out of your house, but you'd keep the monthly stipend.*

We stared at them. *We don't care about the stipend. We want her to have a home*, Jo said.

The Children's Services supervisor pulls her reading glasses off her forehead and points to her case notes. *Our philosophy is that—*

Jo cut her off. *You have your philosophy and we have these children.*

My phone vibrates in my pocket and I pull it out. It's Jo.

He's having another
night terror.
Please come home soon.

                    I will. We're
                    just finishing.

Tell her I love her.

I kneel down to look at my daughter on eye-level. *Hey, sweetheart. That was Baba. She says to tell you that she loves you. She'll come see you next month too.*

My daughter hugs me, hard.

We follow the desk attendant to the waiting area, reach into a large cardboard box dusty with farm dirt, and lift pumpkins onto the table. *Remember when we carved pumpkins together last Halloween?* She doesn't answer.

Mr. --- appears. *Give her that coat,* he says, gesturing toward but not looking at me. *You have one at home.*

My daughter silently hands me the purple jacket then turns to catch up with Mr. --- who's already out the door. Halfway across the parking lot she stops and looks back; I wave in case she can see me. When she reaches the dilapidated mini-van, the engine is already running. She heaves open the door and climbs in. I watch until the van disappears into the night.

I hurl my pumpkin at the ground.

A Piano and a Flute

Jacqueline Guidry

They've been at this bus stop fifteen, no make that twenty minutes, and are both out of sorts, more so than usual. The day is too hot, the air heavy with humidity. Not as bad as it will get in August, but neither of them thinks about the rising misery awaiting them in a few short weeks.

She bends down to scratch an inflamed bug bite on her ankle. Not a mosquito. Lasting too long to be a mosquito. Mite? Bedbug? If it's bedbugs again, she'll start shooting. Bugs first, landlord second. Who else? She considers this, who deserves a bullet from her, and the list isn't as long as it sometimes gets.

The boy wants what he usually wants, to be someplace else. Today that place is back in the apartment with the old-time gangster movies channel he just discovered. Last night, he dreamed he was snatched off the streets, a gang recruit ready to belong to somebody besides his father's half-sister. She never forgets the half part, though he could be her son, they're that much alike. Hair so blonde it's nearly white. Thumbs crooked as if with arthritis, which they don't have. A near constant itch to take off.

His dream had been black-and-white, like the movies, and his surprise at that kept his thumb in his mouth after he woke. She's right about him being too old to thumb suck. He's seven but gets taken for six. That's because he's too skinny, she says. He doesn't suck the thumb when he's awake. How can he control what happens when he's asleep? She agrees no one can control what they do in their sleep and this makes him feel better.

Tonight, he's wrapping scotch tape around and around the offending left thumb, always the left, until he's certain the bulk and the taste will drive the finger out of his mouth, asleep or not. Taking care of that rebel thumb tonight.

"Here's the thing." She steps to the curb, peers down Broadway. No sign of their bus. Must've just missed the last one. Typical, given how her day is going. "You listening or what?" she demands and swivels in his direction.

He slumps against the outside corner of the shelter, folds his arms across his chest, scowls. A cigarette dangling from the corner of his mouth and he'd hit the mark, a perfect junior version of last night's mobster.

She cracks her knuckles, trying to distract herself from the itching about to topple her into the crazy lane. Where is that bus? Is she even pushing for on time? No, she gave up on that. Just show up. She sways in time to music she'd be hearing if her iPod hadn't gone dead two days ago. She's getting another, deserves another. Soon as the next paycheck clears.

"When I was your age, I'd memorized eleven pieces of music," she says suddenly and taps her temple. "In here. Eleven. Played them all."

"Eleven." He is too startled by this new revelation and too impressed by the number to keep his pose.

"Not *Twinkle, Twinkle* crap either. Bach and Beethoven and Mozart. Tough shit."

"Tough," he agrees, the names vaguely familiar. He wants her to keep talking because now he's curious.

She shoves him inside the shelter and he loses interest in Bach and company. "Sun's bad for people like us." She runs fingers through her hair, as thin as his. "Why do I have to keep pounding that into your hard head?"

He presses a thumb along one side of his skull. Harder than everybody else's? Could be.

"You believe that?" she asks. "Bach."

"Mozart." He draws out the "z," wishes he had that sound in his name.

"Beethoven." She completes the trio. "You? What can you say for yourself?"

"I don't have a piano." If he had a piano, no telling what he'd play.

"Piano? Who said anything about a piano? Why are you always making up stuff?" She is next to him now, a hand resting lightly on his shoulder but keeping him right there. "I didn't need a piano. Didn't need a flute. Bet that's what you were saying next. Flute."

He squirms away, glad when she doesn't reach for him again. Now he's the one wishing hard for that bus. Flute? What's he supposed to do with a flute?

She spits on the tips of two fingers, slathers the glob across the ankle bite. "What I need is a Band-Aid. You got a Band-Aid?"

He digs in both pockets of his jeans, hand-me-downs from an older cousin, as if that original owner might've also handed down a Band-Aid. Nothing. The cousin is careful about emptying pockets before sending his discards to the boy. There was the dime wedged in a tiny tear of a pocket, but so far that has been the only exception.

She watches him pull both hands out of his pockets and dangle the lining so she can see he isn't holding out on her. She turns away in disgust, sees no sign of a bus, turns back to the boy who's stuffing the lining back in his pockets.

"I like music." He wets his lips as if preparing to blow a flute. What about a sax? Could he have that instead?

"You like crap. That's what you like."

"That's what you say." He wants to offer a better defense, but nothing comes to him. He admits to playing his father's abandoned CDs too loudly but can't resist filling the room with a sound that isn't him, isn't her. Rhythms pound the floor, the ceiling, the walls, blanking out the rest of the world. Him and the music and nothing else. She's always back too soon, turning down the volume until he barely hears a note. Not that he wants her gone forever. If she left for good, who'd buy the Cocoa Puffs? He loves his Cocoa Puffs.

"And what I say counts," she says.

"One, two, three, four." He can't help the smirk but drops it fast. If somebody else was around, he'd indulge, emboldened by an audience.

"You're so much like him, some days…"

"You can't stand it." The boy beats her to the line that comes next.

"Some people have no luck," she says. How did a week or two watching over the boy end up being close to a year? She needed this on top of cleaning office buildings at night, seeing to sick old people during the day? Where was she supposed to find space for this half-nephew?

He goes to the bench in the shelter, tired of the bus that isn't coming and the heat and the standing. Some days, he finds a discarded newspaper, more rarely a magazine. Not today. Just his luck. Same luck as hers. Same as his mother's, busy getting herself together. Doesn't she say so every time she remembers to call? Same as his father's, wherever he is. He blames all of them for the miserable luck they willed him. He kicks at the screw anchoring the bench to its cement platform and that feels good, so he does it over and over.

She's still standing, staring down the street. Then, she turns to him again, hands on her hips. "Stop that. You want me to get charged for a broken seat?"

How would anybody find out? It's just the two of them.

"Know what I'd do if I won the lottery?"

"Buy a piano?" He isn't messing with her, thinks he'd like to learn piano even if he only played nursery rhymes to start. Later? Later he might tackle Beethoven, Bach, Mozart. If her, why not him?

Like the boy, she thinks of stroking keys, pulling out melodies she faintly remembers from days so long ago, they might've belonged to someone else. Could a person pick up details of a different life, imagine the particulars so exactly that the other life became her life? Had she ever played those composers or had the experience belonged to somebody else? To a character from a forgotten TV series? She shakes her head rapidly, back and forth, but nothing useful is dislodged.

"A piano and a flute," he says. They'd share. Some days, he'd play the one and she the other. Next day, they'd switch. Which would be his favorite? Flute, he decides. You can carry a flute anywhere. If he had a flute right now, he'd play a tune to call the bus to them. "I'd mainly play the flute."

She joins him on the bench, smiles eagerly as if this is a new boy she doesn't recognize, doesn't have to watch over all the time, no end in sight. "I'd like that, you on the flute."

"You on the piano."

"Me on the piano." She strikes imaginary keys and he follows her lead. Their fingers, crooked thumbs and all, dance in the air. This pleases her so much, she grabs his hand, the palm small against hers, and gives a friendly squeeze. Only a boy, she tells herself. Mustn't forget, she tells herself.

A bus appears down Broadway. Theirs? Too far away to tell. "Go on up there." She gives him another shove, gentle this time, and he stands at the edge of the shelter, protected from the sun but able to see down the street. "You catch the number?"

"Not yet."

"You will." His vision is sharper than hers and he'll spot the number before she ever could. "You tell me when you see it."

"I'll tell."

She knows he will too. A good boy. "We'll have ourselves Cocoa Puffs soon as we get home."

"Number five," the boy calls out triumphantly, eager to take full credit for the bus's appearance. He steps to the curb, making sure the driver sees him. If they miss this bus, he can forget the flute, forget the piano. Maybe forget the Puffs too.

She stands behind him, hums. He doesn't recognize the melody. Mozart, he decides, with its "z." He goes completely still, all of him intent on listening, hoping he can repeat the notes when she's not around.

SUMMER SOLSTICE (DOGS OF LIGHT)

VEER FROST

A ramping day, too big, the hours swelling,
fanning out like a movie gang taking over,
like dogs bred by the sun to be this once unchained.
I count three, maybe four,

insomniac eyes not up to their numberless glitter,
fractals of the apotheosis now bounding

into the small wired rooms around my heart, their claws
a star's, igniting fire trails across the tongue
deep into the skin and bone part of the soul
forged by a bunch of unhelpful myths,
whose success is nevertheless quantifiable. Am I a tree

to stand up jubilant, vindicated? The birds have shed
their indigo caution, small splendors
swooping to vie with pure incandescence, with the three
or four now vaulting the sun's way
toward its apex,
the firmament to its geometry of perfection. I was up early,

hoping to go on quietly watering the peas and eating them,
as if no sighing and round-shouldered self might be spun
in this bright flood and tossed out as coal spits out diamonds,
an iota of a radiant, equatorial, phosphored burst.
The rapture of dogs is like no other. Footprints of their lightning
    enter the sun
    as the last photon
    swings the year, scattering
    the blown door of the skies until

    all is the light, wolf-eared, grinning.
       Pet me,
I hear it resound in the infinite mouths of the new summer leaves,
with burning fingers, pet me.

Contributor Comments

Mario Aliberto III, "A Good World"
Mario Aliberto III is a Long Islander posing as a Floridian, as well as a husband and father.
Twitter: @MarioAliberto3
"A Good World" began with a simple premise: A person on the side of the road, and why were they there? From that seed, I couldn't shake a vision of a girl burning her feet walking the yellow highway line under the hot Texas sun. I wanted to know more about this mysterious girl, and who would care for her. That's when I heard the character of Gene Shaw speaking to me about his experience with the girl, and he spoke so loud, I couldn't ignore him. This became Gene's story, and the girl remains a mystery.

Emily Brisse, "Hup"
Emily, a writer and high school English teacher, lives just outside Minneapolis with her family. Connect with her on Instagram at @emilybrisse.
When I returned home that night to a dark house, I didn't care that it was 11:00 p.m. or that my children were sleeping or that I'd be tired the next morning when they woke at 6:00 a.m. I wanted to turn on all the lights. I barged into the bedroom where my husband was reading and kissed him, laughed, told him everything, held out my hands to demonstrate the width of the ladder. I stared at my hands, awed anew at what they'd done—their grip. "Are you drunk?" my husband asked, smiling. For a long time, after finally lying beside him, I felt my body remembering that drop into empty, electric space. I wrote this as a way to keep remembering.

M. Soledad Caballero, "Gravity Haunted"

M. Soledad Caballero, Professor of English at Allegheny College, is a scholar and poet whose work focuses on British Romanticism, interdisciplinarity, and the Cognitive Humanities, and poetry.

This poem is one of fifteen prose sonnets I am working on about my fear of flying. For me, flying is emotionally draining, and it feels simultaneously unnatural and supernatural. Even though I was only a child, I still vividly remember the flight from Chile to Oklahoma, the flight of my immigration to the US. Recently, my husband and I have been rereading the Odyssey together; bodies traveling in that world are at risk and in danger and pain all the time. Traveling in this poem is brutal. This poem emerged out of this rereading and my anxieties about flying.

Ryan Clark, "In the Skies Above Southwest Oklahoma"

Ryan Clark teaches English and Creative Writing at Waldorf University, where he is obsessed with puns and the absurdity of borders.

I was born at Altus Air Force Base. As the son of an Airman who worked on the flight line fueling planes, the base was always meant to be a temporary home, a place to leave. In writing this poem, years and distance removed, I wanted to find where home was for me there, if I could still find it. Could I find a way to fit into its story? What history sticks to a place, and what of a place sticks to us? These are questions I wanted to explore through this poem.

Photo credit: Diana Humble

Tony Dietz, "Stages of Grief"

Tony Dietz is a writer and engineer living in Phoenix. He has been awarded a grant from the Speculative Literature Foundation and has been published in Everything Change, Volume II: An Anthology of Climate Fiction. He can be found at tonydietz.com and @tony_dietz.

"Stages of Grief" came from the furnace heat of a Phoenix summer. The first sentence arrived complete, and the story flowed from there. Looking back, I think I might have been influenced by seeing "The Curious Incident of the Dog in the Night-Time" on Broadway and by my daughter's reaction to the play. I consciously took my character through the five stages of grief following the death of her dog but was surprised when the story turned out to be about her acceptance of a different death, and by the person best able to help her to this acceptance.

Sean Enfield, "Song of the South, Reprise"

Sean Enfield is an MFA student at the University of Alaska-Fairbanks; his work can be found at seanenfield.com. Instagram/twitter: @seanseanclan
Trump has given a new voice to tensions deeply ingrained in our nation, but the racism inherent in his presidency is also inherent to America, itself, hence his nostalgic campaign slogan. This piece started as investigation into a particular manifestation of racism and nostalgia—*Song of the South*, a movie locked in Disney's Vault. My grandmother screened it for me when I was a boy, and the more I researched and wrote about the movie, the more I began to see how my family, interracial as it is, also fit into a legacy of racism and its supportive silences.

Veer Frost, "Summer Solstice (Dogs of Light)"

Veer Frost lives and writes in the Northeast Kingdom of Vermont, absent social media and, too often, internet access. As well as poems, she is the author of a novel under consideration for the Bakwin award, The Child at the End of the World, *and is at work on* Little Book About Dreams.
There is a moment when everything, even nature, seems to conspire against the choices we've made, or perhaps it is a concatenation of such moments that builds to a point. My Summer Solstice poem blew up out of this crossroads in my life as an artist. In spirit, everything talks to the artist, from the pebble to the star. A dream had required me to sign a contract to write and paint, itself a story of doubt and denigration faced off by intense desire. Where conflict is, language fountains up, to obscure and defend as well as illuminate. Jung writes of the sacred "Third" born out of dualities, like a child to parents. I see my Solstice poem as an exploration of a daily process of confronting and embracing who I am.

Henry Goldkamp, "Passive-Aggressive Flotsam Cross"

Henry Goldkamp was born and raised in Saint Louis, Missouri. Recent work appears in Indiana Review, Diagram, South Carolina Review, Lumina, Notre Dame Review, *and* The McNeese Review, *among others. He is recipient of the 2019 Academy of American Poets Award and the Ryan Chighizola Prize from University of New Orleans. His public art projects have been covered by* Time *and* NPR. *Currently, he lives in Louisiana with his small, lovely family. Instagram: @thisbadbeach*

This poem is my current relationship with Catholicism. My lyric treatise against holes in its plot. From the get-go, the idea of dominion over everything (id est Genesis 1:28) leaves that iron taste of hierarchy in my mouth. I lionize the human animal over the human human. Catholicism, it seems to me, smothers this part of us (potentially). The fa(c)t of the matter: There is an animal in me, and I'll be damned if I feel bad for loving her. And ain't no way in hell I'm sacrificing my puppy no matter how many times she pisses on the carpet of my heart.

Jacqueline Guidry, "A Piano and a Flute"

More about Jacqueline and her work can be found at www.jacquelinemguidry.com.

As with much of my work, "A Piano and a Flute" took its own slow time developing. My entry into the story was dialogue between the boy and his caretaker, her claiming to have memorized eleven pieces of music. I can't remember, perhaps never knew, where that image originated but can identify the origins of other elements. Like my characters, I have spent inordinate periods waiting for bus number five. My daughters play piano and flute. At some point, every newsfeed seemed to mention bedbugs. Eventually, as happens when I'm lucky, these and other disparate pieces melded into a whole.

Ashley Hand, "Homecoming"

Ashley Hand is a service academy graduate and spent her career as an Air Force officer deploying around the world. She lives and writes in upstate New York, where she is pursuing an MFA at Cornell University and works as an assistant editor at EPOCH magazine. Find her on Instagram: @ashley.unabridged.

Images of joyous military homecomings can be quite compelling—women in sundresses holding colorful banners, children waving small flags on sticks, dashing heroes scooping loved ones up into their arms. We've altogether mythologized these reunions. As a woman who has been, by turns, the one deployed and the one welcoming a deployed lover home, I meant to pull back the curtain and show that reintegration can in fact be strained and sad and anticlimactic. The story here is in the silence, the things that go unsaid. Special thanks to my longtime mentor Donald Anderson for his guidance and support in getting my writing to print.

Rachel Hinton, "Hydrangea"

Originally from Vermont, Rachel Hinton lives in Chicago, where she works as an editor and teacher.
I had been thinking about the word "esteem" as it had been used in the context of a particular conversation. In myself and others, I notice a sort of flowerlike beauty in that desire for esteem—a fragility and humanness. But that desire is also tangled with other qualities—a pushiness, an impertinence, a link, in our time and place, to money/commerce. I was trying to write more deeply into that tangle of ideas.

Kristen Holt-Browning, "Studies in Erosion"

Kristen is a freelance editor. You can find her at kristenholtbrowning.net, and on Instagram @theholtbrowning.
The piece started with that one word: erosion. I wanted—and still want—to write about the big stuff: death, growing up, growing older, falling apart. But I knew that, in order to do that in any meaningful way, I needed to start somewhere small and precise, so I started with that single word. I write poems too, so I'm often thinking and writing on the micro level, engaging and playing with the word or the phrase. Here, I wanted to transpose that tendency into prose, to see if a different genre might offer me a new way forward.

Photo credit: Valerie Shively

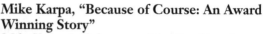

Mike Karpa, "Because of Course: An Award Winning Story"

Mike Karpa (mikekarpa.com) is a San Francisco queer writer whose fiction, memoir and/or novel excerpts have appeared in Tin House, Chaleur, Sixfold *and other literary magazines … and with this story may never again.*

Entering contests brings subscriptions; unread magazines can pile up. Last fall I read through years of esteemed, rejecting magazines. And found no stories by queer authors or about queer people. None. Instead I found characters, settings, elements and plots I've become weary of. In an attempt at catharsis, I channeled them into this meta-story, thinking to set it on fire and push it out to sea. As I wrote, though, I weirdly began to care about the characters. I'm a sucker for imaginary people. This story may even cathart out of me again someday, as a novel.

Kent Kosack, "Origin Stories for the Turtle Lady"

Kent Kosack is a writer and MFA candidate at the University of Pittsburgh where he teaches composition and creative writing. kentkosack.com

My mother was the Turtle Lady, lining up toys on our stoop for me to see when I got home. That nickname is the origin of this story, a story about storytelling, the way we need stories to keep going, to grieve, to connect. The same needs driving the narrator and the Turtle Lady together are what motivate me to read and write.

Darby Levin, "Icarus"

Darby Levin is a Masters student of environmental science at the University of Pennsylvania. When she's not reading or writing about worlds that don't exist, she's rock climbing, camping, and trying to keep up with her Border Collie/Lab mix, Telltail, while hiking.

I have always been drawn to stories based on mythology, and captivated both by flying and the human fascination with flight. In "Icarus," I wanted to write about how a lifetime of imprisonment might have affected someone whose prison was also the only home he'd ever known. And I wanted to explore how such an Icarus would conceive of freedom: the freedom Daedalus imagined, of a new island, or the much more temporary freedom of flying, and of the air.

Victoria Lynne McCoy, "Dispatches from Home"

Victoria Lynne McCoy is a poet based in Los Angeles, and you can find more of her work at www.victorialynnemccoy.com.

This poem began as an admission of failure: a failed erasure project turning news reports about war into love poems, something beautiful. Trying to move on, the idea was stuck in my head—I needed somehow to still create something tender and full of love from them. As I was living in Brooklyn and preparing to visit family in California, I began to see how the Pacific had embedded itself in me. A dear friend was then deployed for a second tour in Iraq. As all of these pieces coincided, I found a different kind of love poem, a bittersweet ode to my childhood home, my childhood friend, my childhood self.   *Photo credit: Alexis Rhone Fancher*

Carrie McGath, "Dear Anhedonia" (AWP Intro Journals Award Winner)

Carrie McGath's collection of poems, Small Murders, *was released in 2006 by New Issues Poetry and Prose. Carrie is working on her second collection and is a doctoral student in the Program for Writers at the University of Illinois at Chicago.*

"Dear Anhedonia" is a poem from my second full-length collection, *The Luck of Anhedonia*. The poem opens up the narrative that will continue throughout the collection between the speaker and the character, Anhedonia. The speaker and Anhedonia (named after the mental illness of melancholia) find solace in one another in the poems and this particular poem illustrates their origin story. Here a reader sees what they are running from and what they are running toward — one another. They are escaping bad lives and relationships for a new life in the desert, a prevalent backdrop in the collection. (For more about the AWP Intro Journals award visit awpwriter.org/contests/intro_jour nals_project_overview.)

Cate McGowan, "Heretic"

Read about Cate and her work at catemcgowan.com.

"Heretic" was born out of anger. A few years ago, I rediscovered a heartbreaking news item about the Senator, a 3500-year-old Florida bald cyprus destroyed by an arsonist (it happened just around the corner). Why would someone kill that tree? I imagined and explored the fire-setter's motivations, her plight. At the time, too, our dear cat, Bocephus, was dying, so my husband often carried the old feline around in a sling to keep him warm. I named my first drafts, "Weird with a Fire." And the story is weird, an admixture of what was around me as I wrote.

John A. Nieves, "On Contrast"

Learn more about John at johnanieves.com.

I was intrigued by the way both cold and heat erase different things. I started thinking about the way we think of cold as death when winter is essentially an incubator in which the days keep getting longer. Summer is a constant cycle of eating and rotting and growth and death and shortening days. I wanted to catch these ideas on a personal level in a kind of meditation where the forced caesuras reinforced what was disappearing. I hoped to capture the emotional poignancy of two simple, echoed moments.

Carolyn Oliver, "Crepuscular Behavior"

Carolyn Oliver lives in Massachusetts with her family; links to her work live at carolynoliver.net.
Twitter/Instagram: @carolynroliver

"Crepuscular Behavior" began when I saw a picture of a cassowary. It's been so long that I've forgotten where I saw it, but I couldn't forget the cassowary's electric blue feathers, its talons, its casque. I read about their diet, their habitat, their fearsome reputation, and listened to recordings of their booming calls. As I pried at the edges of a story about a woman with secrets and mistakes she doesn't share with anyone (anyone human, that is), the cassowary pecked at my attention, until I realized the isolated woman and the huge bird belonged in the same story. *Photo credit: Benjamin Oliver*

F. Daniel Rzicznek, "Lake Reality"

F. Daniel Rzicznek's newest collection of poetry is Settlers (Free Verse Editions/Parlor Press), and he teaches writing at Bowling Green State University in Ohio.

"Lake Reality" stems from an experience I had while fishing with my father and a family friend. A series of rainstorms caught us by surprise, and the resulting afternoon was surreal and uncomfortable in how we were reminded of our smallness and frailty. I wrote the poem with the larger landscape in mind (the sky above the lake, the water and history below, the area surrounding) as a way of highlighting the smallness of the human condition within the immensity of Earthly reality. The title comes from a sign misread on the drive home that day: Lake Realty.

Photo credit: John Jarvis

Jen Sammons, "Visitation"
(AWP Intro Journals Award Winner)

Visit Jen online at www.jensammons.com

This piece began as a writing exercise in a hybrid forms workshop at Miami University this past fall and would have stayed firmly in my computer had it not been for the urging of my professor, TaraShea Nesbit. Writing this piece marks the first time that I have tried to begin to tell the story of what happened to my children at the hands of agencies, organizations, and professionals who claimed to make decisions in the best interest of the child, and is part of a larger manuscript-in-progress about the making, unmaking, and remaking of my family. (For more about the AWP Intro Journals award visit awpwriter.org/contests/intro_journals_project_overview.)

Paige Wallace, "Grandma's Letters" (Ooligan Press 2019 Write to Publish Award Winner)

Paige Wallace (storycatchercreative.com, @storycatchercreative) is an Oregon farm girl who now lives in Portland, where she creates digital content for businesses, writes personal essays for her sanity, and can often be found fly fishing, swing dancing, or practicing tai chi.

My grandmother was my favorite storyteller. She provided warmth and safety I lacked at home, and held that supportive hug around me long after I entered adulthood. I set out to write about the deep connection we developed through our correspondence, and to immerse readers in the times, places, and emotions I experienced throughout this relationship. Writing about Grandma came easily, maybe because my memories of her remain astoundingly vivid, or because she gave me so many words and stories to draw upon. Most importantly, she inspired me to write down the things that matter in life and share them. (For more about Ooligan Press's Write to Publish contest, visit ooligan.pdx.edu/events/writetopublish/contests.)

Mathilda Wheeler, "Sex Ed"

Visit Mathilda at www.thewonderwriter.com
(an occasional blog).
After I received affirmations when "My Mother's Suit" appeared in Into the Void, vol. 3, I accepted more readily that my personal stories have value to others, despite or maybe because of being so normal. The challenge of creative nonfiction based on childhood lies in re-creating "true" memories in scene. I do not trust my memory. As I workshopped "Sex Ed," I found that even simple editing shaped my memory and my interpretation of what happened. It makes me question, "What is truth?"
Something like this happened. The memory I fully trust is the silence I kept about it.

Erik Wilbur, "After Reading Reports from the California Wildfire, Six Weeks Before My Father's Overdose"

Erik Wilbur teaches writing at Mohave Community College in Lake Havasu City, Arizona. Instagram: @erik_othertwin
I couldn't write for months after my father died. I discovered during this time that he'd become the most significant member of my audience in the years leading up to his death. Regardless of content, my poems were spoken in a voice I often imagined him hearing first and were aimed at modeling a poetic attention that brings compassion and gratitude—things I thought would heal him. Then he died, and this project lost its object. This poem—the first I completed after his death—comes from a different place. Perhaps more than any I'd written before it, it's motivated by my own need for poetry. *Photo credit: Cheyennne "Jonnie" Reed*

About the Cover

"Aaron," Leah Goren

I am a California-based illustrator who received my BFA in Illustration from Parsons School of Design in 2012. I primarily work on commercial projects for clients like Anthropologie, ban.do, Penguin Random House, HarperCollins, and the New York Times. My commercial work spans from decorative surface patterns for ceramics, textiles, and homewares, to book covers, advertising, and editorial pieces.

In my free time, I really like to work more loosely and freely in my sketchbook. I don't always have a ton of time for it, but when I do I usually draw my surroundings. I like drawing scenes, especially with people in them. My sketchbook becomes a diary of sorts, where I can look back at days with friends in the park or everyday scenes around the apartment. Sometimes I'll home in on small details, and other times—like the drawing of my cat Aaron on the cover—I challenge myself to draw very quickly and loosely. When I let go of control, interesting things start to happen with the brush and paint.